A Death in Time

Asked by his former employers in London to keep an eye on a senior academic at a conference at a fishing hotel in Scotland, Jarvis finds that mere watching is easy enough, for Professor Benedict, a refugee from Eastern Europe and a controversial figure, appears to have nothing to hide. But various currents surface among the delegates and the calm of a conference in idyllic surroundings is disrupted, especially when one of the delegates is found in the river in what looks like a nasty accident.

It is not the only death. Soon the police are asking searching questions. Jarvis, his cover blown, is drawn into the investigations and finds that it is not only fish which rise to a skilfully floated fly.

FRANCIS LYALL

A Death in Time

COLLINS, 8 GRAFTON STREET, LONDON W1

William Collins Sons & Co. Ltd
London · Glasgow · Sydney · Auckland
Toronto · Johannesburg

First published 1987
© Francis Lyall 1987

British Library Cataloguing in Publication Data

Lyall, Francis
   A death in time.—(Crime Club)
   I. Title
   813'.914[F]   PR6062.Y2/

ISBN 0 00 232123 8

Photoset in Linotron Baskerville by
Rowland Phototypesetting Ltd
Bury St Edmunds, Suffolk
Printed in Great Britain by
William Collins Sons & Co. Ltd, Glasgow

PROLOGUE

The squirrels were on their usual tree, a pine which emerged from a narrow crack in a spur of rock jutting out over a deep, dark pool. Breakfast was the most important task. They sat, stripping their way into cone after cone, nibbling each down to get at the seeds and then dropping the remains, now looking like old-fashioned spinning tops, on to the path that edged its way along about one-third of the way down the gorge, or sometimes, depending on the breeze, into the water some forty or fifty feet below them.

Occasionally, in the course of checking for danger, one or other seemed to stare down at the river whose brown clear water swirled in the cauldron pools and dark pots that formed its channel in the gorge. In the pool directly below, the water heaved and writhed, like marmalade on the bubble, as the current, bloated by recent storms, was forced this way and that through the undercut and worn rock channels. Leaves, brown with long immersion, rose to the surface and vanished back into the depths. Foam, mostly white but with brown scatterings, collected in one or two of the swirls.

It was all very familiar to the squirrels, save for the object that turned and turned in the centre of the roiling water in the pool. Foam, gathering round it, was etching its outline into something which seemed almost familiar—perhaps that was how it attracted their attention—but neither small brain recognized a figure seen several times in the previous days, making its way carefully (as it had thought) along the path below them. Several times they had avoided its attempts to catch a glimpse of them.

By the time the figure was recognized by other passers-by, the squirrels were foraying in the coppice beside the main road a hundred yards away.

ONE: MONDAY

1

Jarvis hummed to himself as he sat on a wooden seat on the edge of the gorge high above the river and watched his quarry. The measures of Bruckner fitted the landscape. There was a magical stillness in the scene—the soft light washing down the birches which dotted the opposite side of the gorge, their green interspersed with one or two darker pines. He took in the strength of the brown rocks, and the sound of the water, foam-flecked from the cataract upstream, chuckling to itself over shingle before lapsing gratefully again into the deeper pools where doubtless some salmon lurked.

He got up and moved over to a smooth rock, almost the size and shape of a bed. He lay back on it and watched the clouds, letting his mind wind down and all his troubles dissolve, as if the rock was a sponge soaking up his tensions. He wished that all his assignments had been as promising as this one. To spend a few days at government expense at a country house merely keeping an eye on someone. It was not even clear what he was to do, whether there was suspicion and no proof, or whether it was thought that something might happen and it would be useful to have someone on hand, or whether there was something entirely different afoot. 'Don't be provocative. Just keep your eyes and ears open.' Those had been the instructions—the only instructions. More like a rest cure than a job, he thought.

The thought made him sit up. A rest cure, indeed, he thought. That could be George Appleby's notion, couldn't it? 'Let's give Jarvis this job. It needs to be done, and perhaps it will bring him back in.'

Then, slowly, he lay back. No. That would not be like George. He had understood his reasons and had let him go. It might be someone else's thinking, Arnold Waterman, for example, or Michaelis. But not George. The call was genuine, of that he was sure. There was a job which needed someone with his cover. That would be the extent of George's concern. If anyone else was hoping for two birds with one stone, they could forget it. In the meantime he would help George, as asked. And have a free holiday.

The cold of the stone got through to him. He went back to his seat. Below, the ghillie was gesturing, acting out his instructions, and Benedict again and again failing to do what was so clearly being recommended. At length Benedict waved angrily or impatiently at the ghillie—Jarvis could not tell which—and the ghillie turned and made his way along the bank and up the steep path which came out just beside Jarvis.

'Fine day, Anderson,' Jarvis greeted him, rising to his feet. 'Much in the river this year?'

'Hallo, Mr Jarvis,' said the other. 'Commander Phillipson said you were to come today. Will you be trying yourself sometime?'

'I'm not sure,' said Jarvis. 'I've just arrived. I haven't yet asked whether there was any space for me on the river. In any event fishing is easier to watch than do. Didn't you get rather tired untangling me last year, and getting hooks out of the ferns and trees?'

The ghillie laughed. 'Aye. You lost a few hooks last year, but there was some promise. Patience is what you need. The touch was coming. This year you'll get it.'

'We'll see,' said Jarvis. 'How have things been this season?'

'Not too bad,' said the ghillie. 'There was a good rain some days ago, and the run started for us soon after. They must have been lying offshore, or in the river-mouth just waiting for it. There's plenty of water now. The linn is fair roaring. You should go along and have a look.'

'I will,' Jarvis promised. 'How's your friend getting on?'

'Him?' The ghillie sniffed slightly. 'He is not bad, but he has not the patience. He thinks he knows it all, and sometimes he is lucky. Often it is as much as he can do to hit the water, while the fish are lying under the bank. He knows what to do, for I have told him, but he does not always manage. But when he strikes, then he is a bonny sight. He plays as well as anyone. Seems to enjoy it. Toying with the fish. But he has not the patience to make a real fisherman.'

The ghillie paused, and looked sideways and back, down to the stocky figure beside the water. Then he turned and smiled. 'I always find,' he said, 'that these foreign gentlemen do not like being told what they are doing wrong. That one would be happier using a can of poison.'

'Or a net?' Jarvis said, grinning.

The other laughed. 'Or a net,' he agreed. Then, after a pause, looking again down at the figure: 'Well, I'd better get on up to the house.'

'Nice to see you again, Mr Anderson,' said Jarvis, as the other left. He looked down at the stocky figure and began to hum again. Then he set off up the gorge. The path, dotted with clumps of nettles and willowherb, lay just on the edge of the drop. He was careless as he walked. An incautious swing of the arm meant a stung hand. He sucked at it as he went.

About sixty yards upstream Jarvis came to the linn. There was a thin cloud of spray rising from the tumbling water, but Jarvis felt he had to get nearer and clambered down the muddy fisher's path to the rocks at the side of the river. Here the rock was conglomerate, with water filling the holes where pebbles and boulders had been eroded out of it. The spray and algæ made progress difficult. He slipped a couple of times, and cursed his thoughtlessness in coming out with smooth-soled shoes when he had heavy-duty shoes back in his room. Their tractor-treads would have helped a lot.

Warily he made his way out on to the promontory rock, his eyes on his footing all the way until he had got there.

He straightened, and only then permitted himself to look up the river. It was as he remembered, but even better, for the river was fuller than he had ever seen it before. He stood and looked, stowing it away in his memory.

It came to him that he collected waterfalls, whatever the technical name for that might be, and that this was a special one. It had never ceased to move him since first he had seen it. One could look up through the narrow linn and see the water the whole length from the upper reaches of the river. Though twisting, the walls of the cut never closed off that view of the lower third of the Key Pool in the higher river above the falls. The contrast of smooth and tumultuous, of the water-shaped walls and the birch-clad banks and fields above the defile, enchanted him. How like life, he thought. The peace of the water of the Key Pool reflecting sky and cloud, and giving way to the peaty brownness of this narrow canyon and the pools and pots of the cascade. There, there was tranquillity. Here, the same water poured up and out, boiling and foaming, from the cavities that obviously under-cut the rock on either side.

Below him, in front, was the final pool, where the water gave one last swirl before becoming again a river instead of a torrent. Sunlight arced into it, and he could see, not far below the surface, three or four large fish. One rose to something. He was not sure if he had heard the 'cloop', but he did see the nose momentarily break surface before the fish returned to its companions, going back exactly where it had been before. The tails moved in unison, keeping the fish motionless with respect to the side walls of the pot. Almost as if they were station-keeping, he said to himself. Then with a flick of its tail, one peeled off from the forma-tion and headed off upstream. It had run the gauntlet of Benedict. Now it was to pit all its strength against the linn.

He looked up through the spray to the quiet flow above the falls. Good luck, he thought, and waved the fish a salute as it disappeared.

2

Above the linn lay the Key Pool. Jarvis walked its length. In the meadow across the river he saw a rabbit or two, and many molehills. The river itself flowed evenly as if resting before the tumult to come. But even so some foam patches were drifting about on it, relics of the higher gorge. These gathered in the lee of rocks, or, caught by the fitful wind, slid sideways across the flow.

Half way up the pool he stopped and listened. There was a peewit somewhere over to the south-east, and the birch leaves made a soft sussurration behind him.

The going became difficult as he came to the muddy area where a side-stream crossed the path. The short detour to a plank bridge had itself become a quagmire, and he edged his way along from tussock to tussock. Even so, he got one foot well muddied when he slipped briefly, just when he thought he was safe. Tractor-treads, he told himself. How could he have been so careless? Too eager to get out?

Back at the river he strode on. At the top of the pool he stopped, and looked back down its length. The path had been rising imperceptibly and he was now some twenty feet above the water. But even knowing that, he was surprised as he looked back to see how low the falls seemed. That drop must explain the force of the cataract, he thought. And also the smallness of the escape from the wideness of the pool. No wonder the water had been able to cut through that ridge of rock which he now saw so clearly lay across the foot of the little valley. Must be like a pressure hose.

The pool itself seemed changeless, the only movement being an occasional swirl and the moving patterns of cloud and sky. The Key Pool. He remembered Anderson's story the day that they had fished it the year before. It was a story he had heard of not a few pools on various rivers. The monk loading himself with a chain as penance, throwing the key into a pool, going on pilgrimage to Rome, there being served with fish and the fish containing the lost key. Briefly he marvelled at the gullibility of men. And yet there was something in the story which spoke to a deep need in everyone. Was there some deeper truth of which that story was a pale reflection? He knew enough now not lightly to dismiss that suggestion. Appleby spoke often of deep patterns which sometimes surfaced.

Jarvis looked back down to the rock ridge which formed? created? caused? the cataract. Where was the next outcrop of that geology? He thought of his instructions, so vague and imprecise. Did someone really expect that he might come up with another outcrop which could link with something else to establish a pattern? Was he seeking conglomerate, or some metamorph?

The path rose and bent to follow the line of the stream. There was mysteriousness here, he thought. Another line of rock crossed the line of the river, but here the rock was more solid than the conglomerate of the lower barrier. He laughed humourlessly as he remembered his recent thoughts. Now he was into metamorphic rock, where the river wound through enormous cracks. It was as if some giant hand had torn the rock to let the water through.

Now the path he was following split, the right-hand path going up into the wood. He took the left-hand path, along the face of the new gorge. This path was cut into the face of the living rock, and even had a small parapet as some protection against the drop down to the dark water. He walked carefully and quietly. As always, a strange solemnity took him on this stretch. There was a hushedness here. The water was too far below and flowing too smoothly despite the swirls to make any noise. The trees were high above him, where the gorge widened, and somehow their noise did not penetrate. It was like a natural cathedral; and yet not natural for his path was made. For years, it was said, French prisoners from the Napoleonic wars had been employed cutting out this path. Half as high again as a man and about four feet wide, it took him up through the gorge. Briefly he thanked them down through the centuries. It must have been an awful task, yet now, so many years later, another could get such pleasure because of their work.

Round the next corner, he knew, was the pine tree above the major pot. He went cautiously, wondering if the squirrels would be there again. The previous year he had seen a pair of red squirrels almost every day on that tree. It had been one of the bonuses, that and the scenery. He had wondered why he had been instructed to go to Ebony House for that week, and nothing had been disclosed. It had just been a good holiday. It had done his ulcer good to be away from everything for a while. This year things were different. Last year had established him. This year he was there for work. But even so, maybe the squirrels would oblige.

They did not. When he rounded the bluff the tree was there as ever, rising high above the pot from that crack. He put his hand briefly against it, saluting it as an old friend. But it was unoccupied. Or was it vacant? He looked at the path and the rock under the main branches, and there was the evidence. His first thought was right. The tree was unoccupied, not vacant. Traces of recent meals were there; shreds of cones, and the odd top-like cores stripped of their seeds and flanges.

He got up on to the rocky spur which jutted out over the pool. As always, he looked at the crack from which the tree sprang, but it was a minor crack. The spur was part of the main bluff. The rock would be secure for centuries yet. He went cautiously to the edge, and looked down.

Here was the most spectacular part of the river, if you knew what you were looking at. From above, it seemed at first that there was no inlet and no outlet to the pool with its dark, apparently endlessly circling, water. He had been told that there was a large crack, wider towards its base, through which the river flowed into the pool, and a similar one through which it flowed out. But the tops of each crack were tiny. Great slabs of rock had slipped sideways in the remote past, and formed this hole. 'The Devil's Plughole', was what someone had christened it, and it certainly played up to the name. And yet that was a modern name, for plugholes were but recent things compared with the scenery in front of him.

The water swirled round and round, a few leaves and bits of foam spinning in the centre of the pot. What else could you call it? he thought as he absently sucked his nettle-stung hand. What would he call it? He thought of flows and circles. His mind skittered off into science fiction. 'The Gravity Well' or 'The Black Hole'? These would do, if you knew what they meant. Then a pun hit him: 'The Pool of Time'/ 'The Pull of Time'. That would do.

He smiled and, returning to the path, went back along it, then turned away up the bluff to the road he knew was nearby.

Dinner would be soon.

3

There were, it seemed, only five guests at Ebony House, though Jarvis knew that would change when the conference party arrived. In the meantime he was grateful for that curious British reserve which does not permit acquaintance-ship too readily to develop between persons who happen to be staying at the same place. He was nodded to when he made his way, somewhat late, into the dining-room—he had been delayed by a broken lace—but that was the extent of the acknowledgement he got from most. Benedict, reading *The Times*, was the only one who did not look up as Jarvis came into the room. A very young maid took his name and showed him to his seat. He was pleased to find he had been allocated a corner table, from which he was able to survey the dining-room.

His table was at the opposite corner from the main door, and the way into the kitchen lay on the other side of the large carved chimney-piece. There were oil paintings of country scenes on each of the walls, and between the two windows which looked out on to the courtyard.

As Jarvis studied the menu he became aware that Benedict was starting to drum with his fingers on the table. The maid was waiting for Jarvis's order, with her back towards Benedict, when Jarvis noticed. That fitted, Jarvis thought. 'Has a high opinion of his own importance, coupled with a vicious tongue. Scots would call it a "good conceit of himself", not wholly ill-founded,' had been the comment in George Appleby's flowing hand.

Sure enough, as the maid, having taken Jarvis's order passed him, Benedict stopped her. 'I ordered my soup some time ago,' he said brusquely.

'Sorry, sir,' she replied. 'I had to get this other gentleman's order.'

Benedict scowled. 'You could have got my soup instead of standing there. My time is important.' The youngster flushed, and hurried off and brought the soup immediately.

Jarvis noted that after this reprimand she hovered around Benedict, bringing him the various stages of his order as soon as she might, and even interrupting the serving of an elderly gentleman in the other corner to fetch Benedict the cheese board.

The result was that Benedict was finished long before anyone else, and left immediately. He seemed to have gone to his room, for Jarvis did not find him either in the library or the lounge.

*

Jarvis decided that he had better report in. Appleby would want to know that he was on the job.

It was a glorious night, cloudless, starry and with a rising moon. He debated taking his car, but decided to go on foot. He went back to his room, got his raincoat, and set off.

As he walked briskly down the twisting beech-lined drive, he at first came close to regretting his decision to walk, for the tunnel formed by the trees was dark and gloomy. The drive itself was sometimes gravel-surfaced, at others merely beaten mud. He wondered if there were any stories about ghosts of the drive, for certainly it would have justified them. Yet once his eyes were accustomed to the gloom, walking down the tunnel striped by moonlight falling between the trunks of the trees was not unpleasant. The leaves rustled in the wind, and he was glad that he had taken his coat. On the left was an open field with several large trees, which from their shapes he deduced to be chestnuts, scattered in it. The further side, he remembered, was another hanger of beeches. It showed silvery in the moonlight. To the right the ground fell away and, down beside the river, tangled rhododendrons formed a pile, black against the moonlight.

He was soon at the gatehouse. Its dark windows made it look unoccupied, but as he drew closer he saw a chink of light and heard the television. He went through the gate, and passed the sign saying EBONY HOUSE. PRIVATE. Then he turned right on to the main road and set off to the bridge over the river and down the mile or so to the village. Long before he got there he could see the orange glow of the sodium lights. Why spoil the countryside with such artificial lighting? he asked himself. The homelier glow of an ordinary bulb, or the even homelier light of gas, would be quite sufficient and would not obtrude. Money, no doubt. Money . . . the root of all evil? No, it was the love of money which was the root of evil. Money. Was that the explanation of Benedict? Or maybe they had got it all wrong.

He stopped at a rise in the road and looked off to the east.

His view was obscured by trees. That was deliberate. He was not supposed to be able to see what he was looking for. Yet over there also he could see the glow of lights. The marvels of science, he thought. Over there was a communications base which, it was said, could listen in to radio traffic within the USSR itself. And heaven knew what else went on within its domes. Why did they light them? Was it so that the spy satellites could get decent photographs? He laughed and, whistling, set off again.

Round a couple more corners and he was into the village. He crossed the square and found the telephone-box.

He dialled, and spoke briefly to the duty officer. There were no messages for him.

On the way back, Jarvis detoured to check the time of services at the church at the back of the village green. Thanks to the sodium, there was just enough light for him to be able to read the notice-board inside the churchyard gate. He was pleased to see that the time of the meeting for prayer the following night would make it possible for him to attend.

As he crossed the bridge, Jarvis stopped to look at the river which lay silver, some fifteen to twenty feet wide between black banks. It was not the classical silver ribbon, but a dappled silver as it moved. Immediately in front of him the channel ran straight for about two hundred yards, before twisting off to the right towards the fishing pools and the linn.

He climbed up on to the parapet of the bridge and sat, dangling his legs over the water. Below him it looked shallow, but he had been told that there were deep pots in the bed, which patches of stiller water seemed to substantiate. A car came along from the village. As it swung round the corner and came on to the bridge, he was briefly illuminated by the headlights. The car roared on. Jarvis wondered if he had been noticed, or whether the occupant or occupants had decided that it was best to mind their own business. It was not every day that one came across someone sitting on the wrong side of the parapet of a bridge.

He sat there for some time more looking at the scene, and lazily picking out such of the constellations as he could remember. There was an unwinking star low to the southwest. He decided it must be a planet—Jupiter or Saturn. He would check. No doubt some of the newspapers would have that information, probably among the weather forecast. But thinking of weather, he shivered. The clear sky was a recipe for lower temperatures. He wondered what the morning would be like. Would the weather hold?

Stiffly, he climbed down from the parapet, and made his way back along the road to the gatehouse, past the sign for Ebony House, and along the tunnel of beeches.

It seemed darker than ever, but, as he told himself, that was a function of the light. The moon was now behind him, and hence did not illuminate as well as before. The dark trunks of the trees were difficult to distinguish against the blackness of the fields and of the tunnel itself.

He was about to start whistling to defy the gloom, when he heard a noise quite a long way behind him. A foot had kicked a stone on one of the gravelled patches. Training took over, and Jarvis stood stock-still, listening. Someone was coming, but the gait was not even. It was as if some three-legged thing was coming. There was a step, a dragging sound and an occasional click.

Jarvis moved off the drive, and stood in deep shadow behind a bush. He turned up the collar of his coat to hide the paleness of his face.

It was difficult to see what was happening. He could discern the approaching figure only as a patch of blackness moving amid blackness, its outline broken by the dappling moonlight. Even when the figure was passing, Jarvis was not absolutely sure what the various noises were. There was a hissing, tuneless moan interspersed with clicks. Then

Jarvis realized: the figure was carrying a stick, and every now and again was striking the ground, or hitting at stones on the driveway. It was also half singing, half humming what the figure probably thought was a tune, and emphasizing the beat with the stick. The peculiar shuffling noise and odd gait was due to a limp, the right foot dragging.

Jarvis realized it was Benedict. He had a club foot. But despite that, obviously he was a walker. Good for him! Still, where had be been? At a pub in the village? That didn't square with his reputation. Or, more interesting, down at the communications base? But in either event, why walk?

Jarvis waited in the shadows for some minutes to let Benedict get well ahead. As he did so, he wryly thought of his previous musings on whether the drive had a ghost. The dark figure of Benedict, its peculiar gait, and the creepy noises, would have persuaded many that the drive was haunted. He laughed inwardly. Perhaps he should go back to the gatehouse and inscribe the Ebony House sign with that Charles Addams cartoon punchline, 'Beware of the Thing'. In a good mood, humming to himself, he set off after Benedict.

As Jarvis came out from the tunnel of trees the older man had stopped near the door, and was looking out over the field in front of the house. He was still there as Jarvis made his way up the small incline to the house itself.

As he came up to him, Jarvis saw that Benedict was leaning on a stout walking-stick held in his right hand. He had a large brown paper parcel under his left arm, and was wearing a black Crombie coat. No wonder he had been so difficult to see back in the drive.

'Fine night,' said Jarvis, coming to a halt beside Benedict.

'Beautiful,' said Benedict. 'But chilly.' He turned for the door. It closed behind him.

Jarvis stayed for a minute or so, listening to the sounds of night. There was now some cloud passing by inland, etched silver by the moon. Suddenly there was a break in it, and Jarvis again saw that planet. He too turned for the warmth, and to search for a newspaper to identify it.

He was right. *The Times* told him that that night Saturn would set at 11.53 pm. 'London time, of course,' he told himself.

TWO: TUESDAY

1

Jarvis was coming out from breakfast the next morning when he bumped into Phillipson.

'Sleep well?' asked the Commander.

'All right for a first night,' said Jarvis. 'It always takes me a couple of nights to get used to a new bed.'

'Fancy some fishing this morning?'

'Well, yes. If there is any free. I was going to book for later on.'

'Good.' Phillipson smiled. 'I remembered you had enjoyed it last year, so when I heard you had phoned I took the liberty of putting you down for a few beats. Just in case there was a rush of bookings. We like to help promising pupils. Shall we?' He gestured to the door.

'You mean with you, not Anderson?' Jarvis queried.

'Yes indeed. Anderson is off upstream today, and I sometimes come out if there is a need. Besides, it will be good to get down by the water on a fine morning like this. I've been trying to cope with staff shortages, and could do with a morning off.'

'Well, fine,' said Jarvis. 'Give me a few minutes to change.'

'Right.' Phillipson nodded. 'Come to the tackle room when you are ready.'

Jarvis changed quickly and made his way out through the courtyard and into the outhouse that served as the tackle room. There he was kitted out with a carbon fibre rod. Phillipson took the flies and a net.

'That's optimistic,' said Jarvis. 'The only ones I hooked last year just grinned at me as they swam away.'

'We'll see about that,' the Commander promised. 'Come on. I think the gaff's in the vestibule.'

'Some vestibule,' said Jarvis in the front hallway, looking round at the vast square chamber. 'It's almost the biggest room in the house.'

Certainly, it was spacious, with a fire built into one side beside the door to the library. The stairs to the upper floor started beside the corridor through to the dining-room and the bar, went up to a catwalk immediately above the main door, and then rose to another catwalk which ran across above the two doors which faced the front door. One of these led to the lounge, and Jarvis knew the one on the left was that of Phillipson's office. Between the doors was an inlaid table with a tall arrangement of dried grasses and leaves in display on it. On the other side from the fire was a large polished wood structure, the product of miscegenation between a coatstand and a sideboard.

'You just wait,' said Phillipson. 'We'll put your salmon in pride of place when we get back.' He pointed to the porcelain platter on top of the sideboard part of the object. At either side, where walking-sticks and umbrellas would have been put in a hatstand, were arranged split-cane rods, musty nets and one or two old gaffs. Phillipson, however, picked up a long dull metal object that lay behind the dish. It looked like a device for immobilizing steering-wheels by running a clamp down to the clutch or brake pedals.

'Here we are,' said Phillipson. 'This is what you need.' He showed it to Jarvis, turning the head and pulling out the telescopic extension. It ran easily until a slight click indicated that it was at its full extension. 'Just get your fish in range of that, and . . .' He gave the gaff a little jerk. Then he collapsed it. It was quite small, about a foot long when shut. 'It's light and handy, but quite strong enough. You can put it in your pocket.'

'Your pockets must be deeper than mine,' Jarvis answered.

'What do you think of our fishing stand?' asked Phillipson.

'It's a remarkable bit of furniture. The sort of thing the second-hand folk would be after to ship to America, though there it would be put to some quite useless use. Ever had anyone after it?'

'Funny you should say that. There was one woman some years ago made quite a song and dance about it. She was a visiting academic from over there—Canada or the States. Apparently she runs some sort of second-hand furniture business on the side. At any rate she tried to get it off me. At first I thought it might be an idea to get rid of the old thing, but she put my back up. Too pushy. So eventually I refused even to put the matter to the Committee.'

'It certainly is a magnificent piece.'

'That wasn't the end of it, though. She got one of the Committee to raise the matter. But that got nowhere. One or two questions soon let the Committee see where the proposal really came from. And I think I was right. It was built for here, you know. We had it out to check for woodworm soon after. The wall behind is original stone, and there are one or two places where the back accommo-dates the stone. No. It'll stay here now, if only to remind me of that woman.' He laughed.

Jarvis raised an eyebrow.

'Oh, she was worth remembering. Now. Where shall we go?' He led Jarvis across to a large-scale Ordnance Survey map of the area, which was fixed to the wall to the right of the door to the lounge. 'These are all open to us,' he said, running his finger along what seemed to Jarvis to be a long line of river.

'Somewhere where I'm not likely to snag a tree, bush or pedestrian,' Jarvis suggested. 'You choose.'

Down at the river, Phillipson showed great patience with his pupil, for which Jarvis was grateful. It is one thing to go out with a ghillie, even one as helpful as Anderson, and seek to learn what you can. It is quite another when the person running the estate takes you out and also shows a flair for teaching which is not blunted by a pupil's errors. There is a limit to the mileage that can be got out of it being 'first time this year' on a river.

Phillipson had chosen to take him to the south bank, below the linn. He took him round by car, across the bridge and then up a cart track, from where they made their way down the other side of the gorge to more or less where Benedict had been fishing the day before. That way, Phillipson said, it would be easier to cast into the north verge of the stream.

It might be for him, thought Jarvis not a few times in the next hour or so, as he cast and cast and cast.

Unfortunately, at one point he erred on quite the wrong side of length, and his hook caught in a branch which was wedged between rocks on the other side of the river. Phillipson said that he would go round and deal with it, and did so, despite Jarvis's protest that it was his fault.

As Jarvis sat gloomily on a rock waiting, Benedict came along the upper path on the other side of the gorge. He had a stout stick in his hand. With it he was smashing down plants that grew at the side of the path. At every second step there was a broad slashing stroke, decapitating first on this side and then on that. Jarvis remembered his nettle-sting, but then felt sorry for them in the wholesale destruction.

As Benedict came opposite where Jarvis was, he stopped and looked down at the figure on the opposite shore, lifted his hand apparently in greeting, and then went on his way, still slashing at whatever came within range. He was out of sight by the time Phillipson had freed Jarvis's line and returned. Jarvis commented on Benedict's progress.

'It was him, was it?' said Phillipson, obviously upset. 'He's spoiled the whole side of that walk. But I should have known. I should have known.'

Jarvis looked his question.

'He was always a brute with a stick,' Phillipson explained. 'Does he come often?'

'Every year for the last four. He comes for the conference which is arriving on Wednesday, but he always gets here on the Sunday previously. It's for a few days' holiday, by his way of it. He does some fishing and some walking, but he doesn't go very far. You might have noticed he has a club foot.' Phillipson laughed grimly. 'Never mention it. He's terribly sensitive about it.'

They fell silent, sitting in the sun. 'What do you do for holidays?' Jarvis asked. Then, ironically, 'Don't tell me you go fishing.'

'As a matter of fact, I do,' said Phillipson with a crooked smile. 'The last couple of years I've gone east. There is some marvellous fishing in the streams that come down from the Carpathians; not the Tatras but off some of the smaller mountains. The fish there have never heard of fly, and come quite easily. The Poles themselves don't really fish.'

'But how on earth do you get there?'

'Fly to Warsaw and then down to Cracow. After that it's easier by bus than by train.'

Jarvis smiled. 'And what do the Customs make of your fishing-gear?'

'They are always very puzzled. Last year the exit Customs made me assemble my rod to satisfy their curiosity. It was that one, I think.' He pointed to the carbon fibre rod Jarvis was holding. 'Maybe they thought it was some new form of radio, and that I had been reporting back to some secret base all the time I was over there. Could have, too. There were a few places down there that were pretty hush-hush.'

'Maybe you were lucky to get out?'

'Not really. I had got them to give me a chit for the rod when I went in, and I just flourished that at them. What I was scared of was that I'ld be asked for export duty on the ground that I had bought it over there. They do that with crystal, you know. On your way out the Customs will ask specifically if you have any crystal, and if you say you have, they demand the receipt and assess you a further export tax.'

'And if you haven't the receipt?'

'I'm told they just value it on the spot and charge you accordingly. The trouble is that they aren't experts, and overvalue to be on the safe side.'

'Moral: anything chargeable should be chitted when you arrive.'

'Yes,' said Phillipson. 'Now. How about you justifying my faith in you? We still need that salmon for your display in the hall.'

Jarvis tried. But failed.

2

That evening, when Jarvis came into the dining-room he was surprised to see Benedict rise and invite him to share his table. Phillipson, seated nearby, also made a gesture of invitation, but too late, and Jarvis took the opportunity offered. What was Benedict like? A closer look would be interesting.

Benedict snapped his fingers, gesturing to the maid. She scurried to bring the place-setting from Jarvis's table. He made to help her, but Benedict waved him airily into a seat and sat down opposite.

'I see you are a fisherman,' he said, as they settled down after mutual introductions.

'Not really,' Jarvis demurred. 'I tried it first last year, and thought I'd have another go this time.'

'Aha,' Benedict exclaimed. 'I thought I detected some inexperience when I passed you this morning.'

'No doubt. I happened to see you yesterday afternoon. You seemed to know what you were doing.'

Benedict smiled, then waved his hand expansively. 'Some times are better than others.'

'I find that gorge difficult,' Jarvis said. 'Since last year I've had a try on more open rivers nearer home, but that gorge is quite different. The wind eddies about. I never quite know whether the fly will get past my ear, let alone into the water.'

Benedict laughed. 'Yes, indeed. You must watch and watch. Always watch. Watch for the wind on the water, and for it in the leaves.'

The girl came for their order. Benedict made a point of requiring that there be no croutons in his onion soup.

'Been fishing long?' asked Jarvis.

Benedict again waved airily. He had speaking hands. 'It is a relaxation.'

'Fly?' Jarvis asked.

'Of course. It is more of a challenge. To float the temptation into just the right position, and see the fish rise to it.'

'It takes a lot of patience and skill.'

'Oh yes, it needs patience. The fly is but one of the elements. To know when to strike. And then to hold a plunging salmon—though some trout give a good account of themselves. It tries and tries, until at last you take it.' He gave a brief twisting pull, as if to gaff something at the side of the table.

'I hate the gaff,' Jarvis said.

'I can understand that. But how else to finally make sure? And then there is what Anderson here calls the priest. The blackjack.'

'I am not sure I enjoy fishing as much as you do. To me, just standing there among all the beauty and trying to get the fly in the water is enough. And I'm quite happy really to net a fish and then let it go. But usually I don't get even that far. Getting the fly taken is nearly beyond me.'

'You will see. As you gain experience you too will come

to enjoy all the rest even more. Even the kill.'

'Perhaps,' said Jarvis.

The soup arrived. Benedict had his taken back to the kitchen to have the croutons removed.

'I told you specifically,' he said to the waitress. 'Do you listen to nothing that is said to you? Are you deaf, or impertinent? My stomach, you know. It does not permit these things nowadays,' he explained to Jarvis.

'You as well?' Jarvis exclaimed. 'I can usually manage them, but sometimes, if I have been working hard, they give me trouble too. Still, the girl does have a lot to remember.'

'This idiot girl. She should know. I told her when I arrived my special requirements. I told her again just now. You heard me.'

'Yes, I know. She is very young.'

'She should not be employed if she cannot remember things like that,' said Benedict, frowning, and then made an effort to change the subject.

'You are not here for the conference?' he asked.

'No. I phoned up recently and was told that there was room, though there was a conference on.'

'Very wise. It will be boring. There will be a few young men trying to make their marks by saying what has not been said before. It never seems to occur to them that their hypotheses may have been considered and rejected long since.'

Jarvis laughed, shaking his head.

'It is true,' said Benedict. 'You are young too, but I can see that you would not be so foolish. By the way, what is your subject?'

'Law.'

The girl brought Benedict's croutonless soup. He ignored her apology, and asked Jarvis, 'What kind of Law?'

Jarvis smiled encouragingly to the girl. Benedict did not notice. His head was bent over the plate.

'Mainly Public Law, Constitutional or International Law and such-like.'

'There you are,' said Benedict. 'There you have a real area of study. With developments happening so that there is no sterility. But consider History or Literature or things like that. Even my own field of Economics. The main seams of the past are worked out, and you get these young terriers pretending that they have found some new reef in areas which others have been over for so long. The new fashion, Structuralism, or some other -ism allows them to paw over the . . . What do you call heaps from coal mines?'

'Bings.'

'Yes. Bings. They paw over the bings left by better men than they, and try to make one believe that they have now the truth, and that all that has gone before was error.'

Jarvis watched Benedict, his accent thickening as excitement took over. 'But do they pretend? Perhaps they really believe in what they do,' he said.

'Nonsense,' said Benedict. 'Nonsense. They seek merely to make a reputation, get promotion, or to make money. And now that there is stress on publication to justify their jobs, for most the urge is just to get into print. So they put forward what has not been put forward in the past merely because it has not been put forward before. Novelty, not cogency, is their search. It does not occur to them that these points have been thought of, but discarded without publication by others already. Until recently one did not need to refute nonsense. It was enough to reject it in one's own mind. One would know sensible men would not expect nonsense even to be mentioned. Now, because it is not in the already literature, it is new and is to be trumpeted. Ach!'

'I suppose that may be true of some, but surely not of very many. And is it a new phenomenon?'

'It is true of almost all the young ones. They are not scholars: they are journalists. It is new in its extent,' said Benedict heavily. 'Oh, there are excuses. There are people looking at curricula vitæ who can only count the number of publications.'

'But surely the publication itself is a mark of quality. Some journals have high prestige.'

'Ach, they used to,' replied Benedict. 'But now there are so many journals started by entrepreneurs who are interested only in the profit. The good ones are going out of existence. Those in charge nowadays have no idea of worthwhile work. The ark has fallen into the hands of the Philistines.'

'Wasn't the result a plague of piles?'

Benedict laughed again. 'You know your Bible, I see. Yes, that will be the way of it. The Philistines will get piles. Dagon will fall and the ark will return to the true Israel, the real scholars.' He paused, then added, leaning forward to look more closely at Jarvis: 'I like you. You have a well-stocked mind. Not many of those are now here.'

Jarvis spread his hands. 'My old Prof used to say I had a butterfly mind. I think of it more as a rag-bag.'

'But good! Good! That is what we need. There are too many specialists, mere *idiots savants*, so keen to gain position.'

'Is it a British disease?'

There was a pause, while Benedict considered the roast lamb which the maid had brought for them. She stood nervously to one side until Benedict waved an abrupt hand, and then asked Jarvis, 'What did you say?'

.'I asked if it were a British disease.'

'No. No. It is all through Western Europe. It came from the United States with their "publish or perish" of the Sixties.'

'But they seem to have survived?'

'The rot spreads more slowly through a large country.'

'How long until Dagon falls?'

'I do not know. In my time it is decline. Ever since that idea that all should have education at a university came in . . . what was the name . . . ?'

'Robbins.'

'Yes. In the Robbins Report. It was all done too quickly. Universities must grow, not be expanded like balloons.'

'Too much hot air?'

'Good. Good. I like that. The touch of malice adds flavour. Yes. There was much hot air. Many were appointed who were not really devoted to their subjects. It was a good salary with little duties. Some did not know they were not scholars, and when they found out—they did not care. They became committee men. Now, they have the power.'

'Have you ever read C. S. Lewis's *The Inner Ring*?' asked Jarvis.

'No. Who is he?'

'He was an English scholar who also wrote about theology. In *The Inner Ring* he talks of those for whom getting into the inner rings of organizations was the aim in life. And he also talks of those who do the real work in any subject.'

'He sounds to talk sense. Can you give me the reference?'

'I'll be happy to.'

'Yes,' said Benedict, laying down knife and fork, the plate cleaned. 'Yes. The real work still has to be done. But not by these.' He gestured dismissively.

They sat in silence while the waitress cleared the plates and brought the dessert.

'Good. Good,' said Benedict. 'You appreciate silence too.'

Jarvis smiled.

'It is important,' Benedict went on. 'Too many want to fill every moment with their prattles. They try to impress at every chance. Instead they weary.'

'It's that hot air we mentioned.'

Benedict chortled, with some gateau in his mouth, and purpled. Jarvis quickly banged him on the back.

'Thank you. Thank you,' said Benedict. 'Your joke came at the wrong time.'

'Sorry.' Jarvis changed the subject, if there was one, and over coffee he ventured a question.

'Forgive me for asking,' he said hesitantly, 'but when did you come to this country?'

'Ah,' said Benedict. 'My accent. Nineteen fifty-six,' he went on. 'The Uprising. It was a chance.'

Jarvis nodded. He wondered what the reaction would be if he said that there were people in London who thought that the 'chance' had not been so much for Benedict to leave Hungary as to enter the West.

'There were too many restrictions there,' Benedict added.

'Memories too?' asked Jarvis. 'The war could not have been pleasant.'

'Pleasant?' said Benedict with incredulity.

Jarvis flinched. Obviously he had hit a button. The point passed, however.

'Pleasant,' Benedict went on, but in a duller tone. 'Look.'

He took off his jacket and rolled up his sleeve. Phillipson, rising to leave the room, brushed against the jacket, knocking it to the floor. He picked it up, and apologized.

'That is all right,' said Benedict. 'I was showing Mr Jarvis my arm. See,' he said, thrusting it out at Jarvis.

The tattoo stood out blue against the white paleness of the aging skin. '176-953-612.'

'Majdanek,' he said.

Jarvis and Phillipson stood, looking at the arm. Then Phillipson excused himself.

Jarvis sat down slowly. 'I see,' he said. 'I apologize.'

'No need,' said Benedict, pulling down the shirtsleeve, and putting his jacket back on.

'No,' Jarvis said. 'It was clumsy of me to bring back such memories.'

Benedict shrugged. Then he said, 'Now, my young butterfly-minded friend: later you will ask yourself a question. How is it that someone from Majdanek comes out of Hungary? The answer is also those memories. It also is why the chance to come West was taken. I come from east of Cracow, but thought to change my country to Hungary to escape those memories. And now I am here. A British man.'

Jarvis nodded. He had a lot to think about. There might be more to this job than Appleby had disclosed. Not that the data might not be in the file, but was the interpretation in the file consistent with what he had just seen? Was he there because of doubts about Benedict? Was Benedict a scout, perhaps? Or a courier? Or just a sensor, reporting on a given area—in his case his University and, no doubt, his colleagues and students?

3

The church was a whitish sketch against the trees behind it, an outline, the merest suggestion of a church. Clearly the picturesqueness of the night before had owed more to the moon and less to the civic sodium than Jarvis had realized. Tonight the majestic pacing of slow clouds cast a gloom in which there was only fitful evidence of the moon. There was one point of light; a lamp on a bracket on the porch in the side of the church. He made his way up the path towards it.

The door in the small porch was shut fast, and there were no lights in the church. However, the light did surely mean that there was something going on. He had not mistaken the evening. Should he go to the right or the left? He turned to look back down the path, to see if anyone were coming whom he might ask.

His attention was taken by the golden glint from a gravestone, and a redness in front of it. He moved over to his right to look at it.

It was a plain and simple gravestone in black granite, with gilded lettering. In front of it was a plain vase with a single, fading red rose in it. The inscription on the stone was:

In Memory of Maria Antonovitch
Widow of Philip Antonovitch.
'I was a stranger and ye took me in.'

There was no date on the stone, nor any indication of the
origin of the deceased. In its simplicity, and with that rose,
there was a poignancy about it, not shared by the more
traditional grave next to it, which cheerfully narrated the
history of a whole family of Taylors, who seemed to have
lived long and useful lives and had all managed to get into
the same plot.

He looked at his watch. It was after half past seven.
Perhaps that was why there was no one around. They had
already started. His choice was made for him, and he
continued on the path he was on, round past the main
church door, and so found himself at the door of a church
hall lying concealed from the village, behind the church
building itself. The door was open, and, as he approached,
he heard, first, a few piano chords and then voices raised in
song.

He went in, and picked up a hymn book from a pile on a
table beside the door. The church hall was small and well-
filled. He scrupled to push his way past a large lady who
seemed to be guarding the back row, and went a little way
down the hall to an aisle seat so that he could stretch his
legs and be comfortable. There, with some success, he sought
to give himself to the singing and the initial prayer.

But during the rest of the meeting Jarvis found himself
thinking again and again of Benedict. He did not want to.
He had not intended to do so. On his way in to the village
he had noticed his mind starting to worry the matter, and
beginning to formulate theories and questions. He had
rigorously thrust these out of his mind. But once the minister, Mr Mackenzie, began to speak, they just would not
keep away. The passage being studied was the sending

of the spies from Kadesh into Canaan in *Numbers* 13 and
14, with cross-references to the spies going into Jericho in
Joshua 2.

Jarvis groaned inwardly, and sought to make the best of
it.

What the man said was sound. There was a need to be
faithful to what God commanded. The spying was ordered
not to decide what to do, for God had already promised all
about that. The spying was more of an encouragement, a
pre-view for the Jews of the Land they were to inherit. Yet
most of the spies, and the people, allowed their fears to get
the better of them. Even though everyone, including the
then inhabitants of the Land, knew what God was going to
do. Forty years on Rahab, the harlot of Jericho, knew
what God intended. But the Jews would not believe. They
second-guessed God, and retreated from the 'front-door'
into Canaan with disastrous results, went back from the
'front-door' into Canaan, and suffered for their lack of faith,
their failure to believe what God had said.

Jarvis found his attention wandering, and the passages
mixing up. If Benedict was a spy sent West, what sort of
report would he have taken back? Would he have encour-
aged or discouraged? Would he have seen any Sons of Anak?
And if so, who were they? Where would he have found
grapes of Eschol so large that two men carried a bunch on
a pole between them? Was he a Joshua, sure that his people
could possess the Land even in the face of strong opposition?
And if he were a Joshua, who was his Caleb? And who
might Rahab be?

By this time the address had moved more to consider the
reconnaissance of Jericho itself, and that triggered other
thoughts in Jarvis's mind. Was Rahab a mole?

If Benedict was under suspicion of recruiting moles from
among his students, was that suspicion not sufficient to
justify a check on his former students who were now in
government? Or even to run a check on all those who had

gone through Bicaster, where he taught. What was the point in running a special surveillance during this particular week? Or was there a permanent or semi-permanent surveillance, and he just one of a series who were watching the man? Why watch him? Was Benedict some sort of link man? Could he really be just a courier? Appleby had said that he made occasional trips back 'home', despite what he had said to Jarvis about his bad memories. The memories could not be that strong. Or were they false, manufactured excuses presented to inquirers curious why he was here? Yet that tattoo . . . ?

The minister was obviously coming to a close. Jarvis wrenched his attention back.

If you know what God wants you to do, do it. Do not ask for reassurance. If it is offered, as the Jews were offered the chance to spy out the Land, accept it as reassurance. Do not let the reassurance deter you from doing what you are commanded to do, as the Israelites had done the first time they got to the border of Canaan. And remember that, humanly speaking, there may be more on your side than you realize. Acknowledge them and their help. Rahab married a prince of Israel.

There was another hymn, and then it was time for prayer. The minister welcomed Jarvis specifically, asking if he were up at Ebony House, and saying it was good to see him. Then he proceeded to give a lot of news, much of it about matters clearly already known to the gathering. Some of it was local, matters of domestic concern. Some of the news came from cyclostyled material from missionaries abroad, some from personal letters, and some from ministers elsewhere in the country. Given Jarvis's frame of mind, he noted especially that there was news of Christians in Eastern Europe from two of the many organizations which took an interest in their welfare.

Then the meeting was opened for prayer.

Jarvis was impressed. There were many voices raised in

prayer. Some prayed for domestic, village matters. Others clearly had a world view, and an intimate knowledge of church work in certain countries.

The flow of prayer increased. Jarvis wanted to take part himself, but kept being forestalled. He just was not quick enough to catch a gap. At one point he did start, but so did someone else who was concerned for a ministerial friend in Glasgow who was having problems with a recalcitrant elder, so Jarvis gave way. When that prayer ended, he was about to start again when a known voice clipped in. It was Commander Phillipson. He prayed for Eastern Europe, particularly Poland and the Soviet Union. His prayer went well beyond the information given that night. Obviously, these were of particular interest to him.

At the end of the meeting Jarvis would have had a word with the minister, but an elderly lady got down to the front before Jarvis moved. Then a hand descended on his shoulder, and Phillipson offered him a lift back to Ebony House.

'Nice to see you there tonight,' said Phillipson, as he backed his car and drove round to the street.

'I always go if there is something around,' Jarvis said.

'Good. I was interested to hear you are a member of Mr Giles's church. I have benefited a lot from his writing.'

'You'll need to come and see us sometime,' Jarvis suggested.

'Yes,' said Phillipson. 'I've thought of that a few times. But holidays tend to take me south or abroad. The weather's better.'

'Too true,' Jarvis agreed. 'But a weekend wouldn't hurt.'

'Perhaps. Did you enjoy tonight?'

'Do you mean here or there?' Jarvis pointed a thumb back to the church and then a finger forward up the road.

'Both.'

'Tonight was interesting. It's good to come in among like-minded people. I was impressed by the flow of prayer.

Remarkable to have so many folk out, and so little pause between prayer. I'm not very good at getting started, and got pipped several times, including by you.'

'Yes,' said Phillipson. 'It's not bad for a village. It's all been Mr Mackenzie's doing. He came some six or seven years ago, soon after I did myself. And something happened. He started straight preaching, not too long at first, but interesting. My mother used to come. One wet day I ran her down to the service and came in. I've been coming ever since.'

'Long sermons?' asked Jarvis.

'Some say so. You don't really notice. Your capacity increases. The morning sermon is now about forty minutes, to quarter to twelve. We start at ten-thirty because there is a linked charge a couple of miles away, and its service starts at twelve-fifteen. The evening sermon runs anything up to an hour.'

'That must have taken some getting used to if it was new to the congregation.'

'Yes, it did. I remember hearing about this awful minister that had come, and how he would empty the place. The odd thing is that he didn't.'

'So I see,' said Jarvis.

'Yes, he was a change from his predecessor. He had bored the place empty with dreary anecdotes. When Mr Mackenzie came he just started to tell the people about Christ. That was something Cox had not done for years. He was interested only in his committees.'

'They say that many useless men seek refuge from failure in church committees. There's even a church report which more or less says that. More politely, of course.'

'Old Cox certainly did that. But Mackenzie has made the congregation into a real family simply through preaching his way through the Testaments. It seems to work. Certainly it has been for our benefit.'

He turned the car into the drive to Ebony House, and

they moved gently along the tunnel made by the beeches and the headlights. Faster would have tested the suspension.

'You have an interest in Eastern Europe,' Jarvis said.

'Oh yes,' said Phillipson. 'Those poor people over there, persecuted for the faith which we here seem to despise.'

'It's a great problem. One of the outfits your minister read from seems to me to be barely legal in what it does.'

Phillipson snorted. 'We must obey God rather than man.'

'That can be abused.'

'So can any text. We must help our brethren. It is our duty.'

'Agreed. But some of the wilder folk here put those over there in jeopardy, you know, simply by talking of underground movements, and by smuggling.'

'I've heard that,' said Phillipson. 'I don't believe it. It is in the will of God. Remember Kadesh Barnea.'

The car scrunched to a halt on the gravel outside the front door of Ebony House.

'Would you like a lift to the service on Sunday morning?' Phillipson asked.

Jarvis accepted gratefully.

THREE: WEDNESDAY

1

The next day was the gathering day for the conference. Jarvis spent the afternoon fishing, unsuccessfully but very relaxingly, with Anderson as ghillie.

Things went well for a while, and he played a couple of fish. In both instances, however, he failed to keep tension on the line until the fish had been brought within range of the gaff.

Then he struck problems. No matter what the advice, the fly would not obey him. More accurately, he thought, he had not yet mastered the technique, that easy flick of the wrist. As Anderson—eloquent about his favourite occupation—said, Jarvis's style was closer to that of a flagellant. Twice he got the fly stuck in his clothing, each time puncturing skin.

'I thought I had it,' he complained to Anderson.

'That'll be the trouble,' came the reply. 'When you think you have it, you start trying to do things, and it all goes again.'

'Just like my golf,' complained Jarvis. Anderson laughed.

As the afternoon wore on Jarvis became conscious of a number of passers-by on the edge of the gorge, some watching his antics with undisguised interest, others diplomatically turning their heads as he looked up.

'Never mind them,' snorted Anderson. 'None of them could get the fly into the water, let alone float it. Just relax, man. Relax.'

But it was no good. Jarvis grew more and more conscious of an audience, and decided to give up.

As he reached the top of the path his heart turned over.

He was confronted by a dark-haired girl closely resembling Patricia, the one girl who might have become his wife. But that thought fled as she spoke.

'Had a good day?' she inquired.

'Never ask a fisherman that,' said her companion gruffly, taking her by the arm. He did not seem pleased by her friendliness.

'Tolerable,' said Jarvis. 'But nothing to show for it.'

The girl smiled, and allowed herself to be led off.

Back at Ebony House there was now a row of cars parked at right-angles to the wall on either side of the front door. As Jarvis arrived another two cars came fast up the drive, the second nearly colliding with the first as it stopped, skidding slightly on the gravel. The first driver got out and came over to the second.

'See,' she said. 'You owe me ten pounds.'

A hand held a note out of the window. The woman seized the note and went off waving it in triumph.

'That means you buy the drinks tonight,' shouted the driver of the second car.

'Only as long as this lasts,' she called back over her shoulder.

When Jarvis came into the dining-room he was greeted by a burst of chatter. The place seemed over-full, but his table in the corner was free, and he made his way over to it. Benedict nodded to him as he went past. The other seat at Benedict's table was occupied by an elderly man to whom Benedict was talking in an earnest manner, pointing to something on a sheet of paper.

From his vantage-point Jarvis could survey the room. So this was the conference. It was depressingly akin to so many other academic conferences. Four of the older men present were talking amicably round one of the tables. Benedict and his friend were engrossed. At another table a senior man was either being flattered by the attentions of juniors, or he was seeking to impress. Jarvis was not sure which.

Tables had been put together to form two long tables down the middle of the room. At these were mostly the younger element, noisily talking among themselves, outrageous remarks drifting tantalizingly, audible enough to intrigue. Obviously the ten-pound note and at least one other of its kind had been disposed of to the advantage of several at one of the tables. Seated among these larger groups were three or four more grizzled academics; 'brindled' was the adjective that occurred to Jarvis to describe one in particular.

Looking around him, Jarvis marvelled again at the diversity of types, then laughed out loud as memory crossed his mind. One day he had been sitting with a colleague, now, alas, deceased. A linguist had been present, who had discovered that a lawyer had recently been appointed some way up the salary scale. She considered that unfair. She had had to start at the bottom. Neil had leant forward, and with great deliberation had tapped his pipe on the ashtray and then scoured its bowl with his knife, all the while looking at her. The silence had expanded. Then Neil had asked gently, 'Pray tell, me, madam: are you otherwise employable?'

One or two heads turned to regard the curious fellow in the corner, who had started to laugh, while seated all on his own. Conversation in his immediate vicinity lagged, and then reasserted itself as the demands of politeness were acceded to. Jarvis straightened his face, and held his gaze on his plate for a while, before resuming his inspection.

As he surveyed the dining-room again, he had the same feeling that he had had as Neil had dropped his bomb, a mixture of sheer mischievousness and recognition that a note of truth had been sounded. How many of these were employable? He wondered what Benedict's answer to that question would be. Perhaps he would have a chance to ask.

It was a curious thing that so many were unemployable in anything other than what they were at present doing. Of course the question was now being asked whether they were any good at what they were doing. And was their ostensible employment what they were actually devoting their attention and effort to? Even on a statistical basis Jarvis had no doubt that some of those present had their lectures written and were more interested in something else, hill-walking or the cultivation of their gardens, good works or lechery. And what of Benedict? Benedict was well-known as a scholar, but was that his real occupation, or was his real purpose in life acting as a 'scout'? And if so, how many had he recruited? The imagery took over, and Jarvis found himself brooding about options, free transfers, transfer fees, training and the like.

From that he went off into a brown study. Was he any different? He had messed up one career and, though he was making a name in the new, was he himself otherwise employable? And was his employment only ostensible? Here he was back at his old game, watching. Or was he stalking? Or was ·he fishing? And if he was fishing, was he any good at it? Surely he really needed the help of a ghillie. And who might that be? George Appleby? Michaelis? Waterman?

'Some days are like that,' said a deep voice beside him, and Jarvis looked up into a smile. 'If you are finished, I would like you to come through with us. I want you to meet Professor Milton.'

Jarvis meekly swallowed the remains of his coffee, and trotted after Benedict.

2

In the lounge Benedict and Milton settled into a large settee at one side of the fire, while Jarvis pulled an easy chair to within speaking distance. The two older men had brought drinks with them from the dining-room, so Jarvis went through to the bar and came back with a Canada Dry with ice. Milton looked at it over the top of half-spectacles, and snorted.

'Ginger ale,' said Jarvis, who had long since discovered that it was better to face disapproval of his drinking preferences head on. He pointed at Milton's tumbler. 'I don't like that stuff except with sugar and hot water when I have a bad cold.'

Milton recoiled. Clearly he smelled heresy, if not blasphemy.

Benedict chuckled. 'Old friend,' he said, 'old friend, do not dismiss this young man. I detect in him a shrewdness which I have seen in not many of his contemporaries. He does not say all he knows. He does not speak all of himself, like the many. He is watching us, there, far behind his eyes.'

Benedict turned, and looked directly into Jarvis's eyes. Jarvis dropped his.

'You see,' continued Benedict, turning again to Milton. 'I have him. He is a spy, sent from our lords and masters in London to see whether we are properly stewarding the benefactions they have showered on us. Are we worth their money?'

Milton started swirling his whisky in its glass, looking down into it. Benedict turned again, with a smile to Jarvis.

'True, is it not? You are a spy.'

Jarvis found himself colouring. Was this as innocent as it sounded? Was it badinage or challenge? He decided to play along.

'It may be my duty to send an anonymous letter to the University Grants Committee,' he smiled. 'But so far there are no facts, only impressions.'

'And the impressions?' asked Milton.

'I couldn't help wondering through there in the dining-room, how many of the gathering were employable in real life,' said Jarvis simply.

Milton looked round the room. His face cracked into a wintry smile.

'We may soon find out,' he said.

There was a pause, then he continued, 'Benedict tells me you are a lawyer. At least the vultures will never lack a meal.'

Jarvis acknowledged the hit. 'It is a pity that my profession can make a lot of money out of the misfortunes of others. But we are useful at other times too.'

'What I find difficult,' said Milton, 'is that your profession is clearly very bright, but so many spend their intellects on unproductive matters. Setting up schemes to evade taxes is not a worthy occupation, except for scoundrels.'

Jarvis became conscious that Benedict was sitting back, watching him talk to Milton.

'I agree,' he said. 'But that is in part at least the fault of our tax system. It ought to be possible to establish a simpler tax structure, with fewer holes in it. That is the task of your people as well as mine.'

'Do you think a cast-iron system is possible?' returned Milton.

'No,' replied Jarvis. 'Any system will have anomalies, and there are always those who will pay well for a guide through whatever loopholes may exist. That said, I must also claim that there is a distinction between tax avoidance and tax evasion.'

'And what is that?' said Milton.

'There was a Scottish judge—Clyde, if I remember right— who said that it was not the duty of a taxpayer so to order his affairs that the Inland Revenue could put its largest shovel into his coffers.'

Milton smiled. 'You sound like my accountant.'

'In that case you must yield the point.'

Milton gracefully turned his hand, indicating concession. 'Benedict tells me you are here on holiday.'

'Yes, I was needing a break, and phoned on the off-chance. I gather I got a cancellation.'

'Well, really you are doing us a favour,' said Milton. 'We had booked all the rooms we could but Merrick from Worcester has had a stroke . . . I'm not sure if we would have had to pay the room in any case . . .' He turned, questioning, to Benedict.

'I do not think so,' said Benedict, and went on: 'Bad news about Merrick. I've told him for years that he does too much. He cannot turn down anyone with a two-one who can get the cash to do a thesis with him. It's not as if he needs the money, and it wouldn't go to him in any case. And the department there is not under threat.'

'Maybe he's just the traditional type,' said Jarvis quietly.

'Yes, he is. That is exactly it,' said Benedict, waving a hand dismissively. 'He keeps on saying that it is his duty to the subject to supervise as many as he can. But there are limits. I don't take on more than I can do without running my health down. PhD people can be so demanding. Some doctoralists will take no advice, yet demand evidence that you have read every word. You do not have to read every word to detect rubbish. Criticize and they go in—what do you call it? . . . Huff, yes, they go in huff.'

'Into a huff,' said Milton absently.

'Worse, too,' said Benedict. 'I had one a year or so ago who got so upset that he killed himself.'

'Nasty,' said Jarvis.

'Immature,' said Benedict. 'I should have realized when I saw his first draft. It was juvenile. But he spent so long justifying himself against the little I said on his first written submission, I should have realized he would take stronger criticism badly.'

'It must have been awful for you,' Jarvis sympathized.

Benedict waved his hand, and changed the subject.

'Might I propose,' he said to Milton, 'that Mr Jarvis be allowed to attend such of our sessions as he might wish?'

'Surely,' said Milton. 'Are you interested in Economics, Mr Jarvis?'

'I don't know very much about it. But it is an interesting field of study. It has an interface with Law, and it is on that interface of subjects that one often finds the most stimulating ideas.'

'Interfaces, interfaces,' said Milton. 'For my sins I am on our Equipment Committee. We have just been doing next year's allocations. Everyone seems to want interfaces. I asked if that were a new dress. Vastly offended our History Prof . . . She's a woman,' he explained to Jarvis.

'Ah, discrimination. There's a growth area,' Jarvis murmured.

'More vultures who have the diabolical cheek to tell you it is for your own good,' said Milton. 'Bunch of misfits. Can't run their own lives properly, so they set themselves up to sort out the difficulties of others.' The whisky was clearly having an effect.

'Shaw,' said Benedict.

'Pardon,' said Milton.

'Shaw,' said Benedict. 'Your Shaw, George Bernard. "Then as can, do. Them as can't, teach."'

'And them as can't teach, teach the teachers,' said Jarvis.

The group in the window looked at the three laughing together. 'Pigs,' said one. 'The flower of scholarship,' said another girl, and lapsed into giggles.

3

Some time after one in the morning Jarvis woke. There was a banging in the corridor outside his room. He lay hoping that the noise would cease. Instead the banging became a monotonous pounding, counterpointing what Jarvis assumed must be words. Wearily he got up to investigate, pulling on a dressing-gown as he went.

He poked his head out of his door. Two doors down and on the opposite side of the corridor a figure was leaning against the door, its head couched in the crook of its left arm, and beating on the door with its clenched right fist. Whatever was being said was quite impossible to make out.

Jarvis ducked back into his room to consider. This was most probably the drunken result of the evening, and his first reaction was not to get involved. It was a matter for the conference organizers, or indeed for Phillipson.

Jarvis went back to his door and looked out again. Just then the door opposite his opened. A tousled head appeared. 'Should we do something?' asked Jarvis.

'It's Earlston trying to get into Kate's room,' said the head.

'He's slow in getting the message.'

The other laughed. 'He doesn't think too straight where she's concerned.'

'If I don't get some sleep I'll not think too straight myself,' Jarvis said.

'Has it been going on a while?'

'Yes,' said Jarvis feelingly.

'Oh dear,' said the head. Then it added, 'Wait a mo',' and disappeared back into its room.

'We'd better do something,' said the man, appearing again. Now dressed in what appeared to Jarvis to be a kimono, he came out into the corridor. 'If Milton gets to hear of this it will finish him,' he added.

Jarvis lifted an eyebrow. 'It happens often?'

'Regularly.'

'Perhaps Milton knows, then.'

The other shrugged, and set off towards Earlston. Jarvis followed.

The man put his hand on Earlston's shoulder. 'Come on now, Jack,' he said. 'It's time we were all in bed.'

Earlston straightened. Jarvis recognized him as the man from the riverbank that morning.

Clumsily Earlston struck out at both men. 'Bed,' he said. 'Bed,' with a rising inflection. '*He*'s in there.' He turned and pointed to the door. Clearly he was drunk.

'Who?' asked Jarvis.

'Ssh,' said the other man, trying again to put his arm round Earlston's shoulder.

Earlston swung round again. 'That . . . that . . .' he began, speaking to Jarvis.

'There, there,' said the other man, consolingly. 'I'm sure you've got it wrong. Kate isn't like that. Come on. I'll see you to your room.'

The two set off along the corridor, Earlston arguing incoherently, but allowing himself to be led away. Jarvis watched them round the corner at the end of the corridor.

He was just turning to go back to his own room when the door that Earlston had been hammering on was opened. The dark-haired girl from the riverbank looked out.

'Has he gone?'

'I think so,' Jarvis replied. 'The fellow opposite me has taken him off to his room.'

'Thank you,' she said. 'I'm sorry you've been disturbed, but I didn't dare open my door.'

'That's all right.' Jarvis made to go back to his room.

'Wait,' said the girl.

Jarvis turned back.

She was starting to blush. 'You don't know me, but I would hate for you to get the wrong impression. I'm quite alone here.'

She was becoming embarrassed, but Jarvis was not sure how to help.

'We were once engaged . . . for a few months. And he thinks we still are. Now when I talk to anyone else he thinks there is something afoot,' she finished in a rush.

'Obviously you weren't clear enough.' Jarvis spoke roughly. Despite her accent, she did remind him strongly of Pat, and he resented it. He still felt responsible for her death.

'No,' she said. 'It's beyond that. He doesn't accept it, and broods and every so often there is an explosion, but it never clears the air.'

Jarvis stood, helpless. How had he suddenly become father-confessor? He was saved by the return of the other man.

'So help me, Kate,' he said as he came along the corridor, 'if you don't get things settled with Jack, I'll beat you up myself.'

'I'm sorry,' she replied. 'I was just trying to explain to this gentleman what it was all about.'

The man stuck out his hand. 'Name's Dunne.'

Jarvis shook the offered hand. 'Jarvis,' he responded. Then he added, 'Which kind are you: boots, *An Experiment in Time*, or a letter to a debtor?'

'Time,' said the other, smiling. 'But no relation. And this—' he turned to the girl—'is Kate Greenway. Doctor of Philosophy despite her looks, and the centre of John Earlston's life, thoughts and ambition.'

She held out her hand and Jarvis shook it. Their touch was enough to dispel his unsettlement. Her small hand was limp in his—how unlike the strength that Pat had had. A wintry smile crossed his face, puzzling the girl, who felt she had somehow failed a test, but had no inkling of what it might be.

'I'm serious,' Dunne said to the girl. 'We have all had enough of your love-sick swain. And it's doing him no good either.'

'What am I supposed to do?' she replied with a flash of anger. 'I've told him time and again that I will not marry him, but he won't accept it.'

'Why don't you marry him, then?' said Jarvis, with a grin.

'He doesn't want a wife. He wants a mother.'

Jarvis shrugged, unwilling to get into further trouble.

'You shouldn't encourage him,' said Dunne.

'I don't.'

'Look,' came the exasperated reply, 'you go walks with him. You sit and talk to him.'

'He talks to me,' she said, her lips tightening and eyes starting to brighten.

'That's no way to put him off,' replied Dunne. 'Mines are not the only things with proximity fuses. You would be best just to cut him off. I bet he thinks he fascinates you.'

'Rubbish!'

'Then how do you explain this?' Dunne waved at the corridor.

She was silent. Jarvis thought she was biting her lip.

'Well, I'm going to bed, I need my beauty sleep.' Dunne turned to Jarvis. 'I hope you'll be my witness that I gave this idiotic female some damn good advice tonight,' he said, and moved off down the corridor.

Jarvis was about to follow him when he saw the look in the girl's eye as she watched the retreating back. He wondered if Dunne had any inkling of an alternative reason for Earlston's disfavour with her.

FOUR: THURSDAY

1

Next morning it rained. Jarvis got up and looked out of his window as usual. He saw Benedict limping his way down the path to the river, head bent against the rain as it swept across the fields, stick swinging, decapitating nettles and willow-herb.

Jarvis was half way through his cornflakes when Dunne came into the dining-room. He helped himself from the buffet and crossed to Jarvis's table.

'Can I join you?'

'Surely.'

Dunne sat down, and fiddled with his spoon. Then he looked up. Jarvis waited.

'I'm sorry about last night.'

'Not your fault.'

'In theory, true, but I do feel you are due an apology.'

'If that's true, it is not due from you.'

'I know, I know. But Jack is such an odd fish, and I wanted to explain.'

'Your friend explained before you came back.'

'Oh,' said Dunne. 'Did she? I wonder if she gave you the whole story.'

'I wouldn't know about that. She said they had been engaged, that she had broken it off and that the door-banger wouldn't accept it.'

'Trust Kate to put a better face on it.' Dunne got on with his cornflakes. Jarvis buttered his toast.

'The trouble is,' said Dunne at last, 'that Jack is not thinking quite right just now, and he is under a lot of strain.'

'Who isn't in these times?' said Jarvis unhelpfully. He did not really want to be pressed into service again as a repository of confidences. Benedict was his quarry, yet everyone else seemed to be in the business of uncumbering either their own or someone else's soul. But Dunne did not take the signal, and pressed on.

'I started at Trail University a couple of years before Jack did. He was a dodgy appointment, in my opinion.'

Jarvis raised an eyebrow.

'It was touch and go. Leith let that slip later when the troubles started.'

'Leith?'

'The Head of Department. Or rather Acting Head. It was the interregnum before Nicholls came, and I gather that the Vice-Chancellor swayed things for some reason.'

'That can happen.'

'Jack started a doctorate as well as preparing for lectures. It was pretty awful. Caligula booted it into touch.'

'Caligula?'

'Oh, of course. Sorry. That's the way we refer to Benedict. He was one of the external examiners on Jack's thesis, though one gathers that the decision was unanimous. And I can't say I blame them. Jack showed me the thing, and it was terrible. He just heaps things up with almost no organization and little insight. Substitutes volume for analysis, and isn't always right even in factual terms.'

'So why is he still employed? What about probation?'

'The thesis was still pending. I suppose his supervisor had reported satisfactory progress to that point. He got through on teaching presumably, though there were complaints, but not perhaps to Nicholls.'

'A rejected thesis must be a blow.'

'Quite. He took it very hard. Not officially. There was no appeal, but he took to locking himself in his room. He used to spend time daydreaming before that. I think he saw himself doing something fundamental in Economics . . .

an economic Einstein . . . Nobel Prize and all that.'

'And Miss Greenway?' prompted Jarvis.

'Kate came the year before the débâcle. Jack took a shine to her. She was like a ray of sunshine in the corridor.' He paused, clearly allowing memories time to play.

'He pursued her,' he resumed. 'He was forever in her room about this and that, and he got her to co-author an article. Just to give him an excuse, I think. But that didn't last past the thesis disaster. He withdrew from everyone, except Kate. Then one day he came into my room—he hadn't been in for ages—and said they were engaged. I challenged her and she said they weren't, but she didn't deny it when he turned up with her in the Common Room. According to her, she was trying to help keep him in touch with reality. I told her that was stupid and that he needed more help than she could give, but she went on trying. I left shortly afterwards and have just seen them twice at these conferences. I write to Kate now and then.'

'They didn't marry?' asked Jarvis.

'No. But she still allows him to tag along. Every so often he goes into some sort of decline . . . turns suspicious of anyone she talks to . . . and there's a scene. I think she thinks he will do something dreadful if she cuts him off.'

'To her or himself?' asked Jarvis, interested despite himself.

'Himself, I think. But I wouldn't know. I wish he would go jump in that river down there.' He nodded in the direction of the linn. 'He's too much trouble.'

'Why did you leave Trail?' asked Jarvis.

'Money,' came the swift reply. Then, more consideredly, 'There was this post at Bannerman, a senior lectureship. It was an opportunity. There aren't too many of them going around now.'

'No,' said Jarvis.

'Also I wanted the change.'

'And Miss Greenway?'

Dunne coloured under Jarvis's gaze. 'She's still there.'

'Difficult,' said Jarvis. 'I gather that last night is part of the pattern.'

'Quite.'

'Will it happen again?'

'I hope not, but you never know.'

'What sets him off?'

'I don't know. He churns over things until finally he explodes. Huntley's the most recent hate object.'

'Huntley?'

Dunne looked round. 'That one over there, in the green sports jacket.' He pointed with his spoon. The person indicated was the one Jarvis had thought of as 'brindled' the night before.

'Any truth in it?'

'Don't know,' said Dunne. 'She has a knack of making friends.'

He pushed his plate away and selected a piece of toast. 'But look, I'm sorry to have dropped all that on you. It was just that last night must have seemed very odd to you.'

'I'm in the academic game myself,' Jarvis admitted. 'Every faculty seems to have a few oddities in it.'

'University as asylum,' Dunne said, smiling.

'Home for unemployables,' said Jarvis, the merest flicker of an eyebrow indicating 'joke'.

Just then the door opened and Kate Greenway came in. She came straight across to where Dunne and Jarvis were sitting. Jarvis stood.

Dunne merely waved a hand. 'Pull up a plank. We were just talking about you.'

She frowned. Jarvis swivelled a chair from the next table for her and she sat down.

'No cornflakes?' said Dunne quizzically. 'Ricicles? All-Bran? Brillo pads? Stewed lawn-mowings? Kippers?'

'Shut up,' she said, and turned to Jarvis. 'I don't know what he's been saying to you—'

'Only the truth, my dear. Mr . . . Mr . . .'

'Jarvis,' Jarvis assisted.

'Mr Jarvis deserves some explanation. After all, he was remarkably polite last night. In circumstances of some difficulty.'

'Please excuse this moron,' the girl apologized. 'He knows nothing. But I'm sorry my friend woke you last night. He was under the weather.'

'Rubbish,' said Dunne forcefully, leaning forward over the table. 'The man's nuts. To go banging on a door like that in the middle of the night . . .'

'I thought he was drunk,' said Jarvis.

'He's a teetotaller, with regular lapses,' said Dunne, leaning back.

Jarvis looked at the girl. 'It's true,' she said. 'It was just as I said. He thought I had someone with me.'

'Did you?' asked Dunne.

She rose to her feet, her cheeks flushed. 'Excuse me,' she said to Jarvis, and left the room.

'That was uncalled for,' Jarvis protested.

Dunne sighed. 'Me and my big mouth.'

2

The rain had not improved. Jarvis was standing at the front door when Benedict spoke behind him.

'If you do not possess diving suiting, why not come to this morning's session?'

Another belt of rain swept across the fields.

'Thanks,' said Jarvis. 'I will.'

Benedict nodded. 'Excellent. Come. I will introduce you.'

When they went into the lounge Jarvis's first thought was that they had entered some time stasis device. Everyone seemed frozen, turning towards two figures standing in the window bay. It was Earlston and the brindled figure of Huntley.

Huntley spoke into the silence, deliberately articulating his words, it seemed, so that everyone could hear.

'I suggest,' he said, 'that Dr Greenway's business is her business, and that my affairs, with or without an "e", are of no concern to a has-been like you.'

Earlston hunched his shoulders for a second, then seemed to grow as he straightened himself. He was the same height as Huntley bar an inch.

'Take that back,' he said.

Huntley paused, clearly enjoying the situation. Then he drawled, 'Yes. I take it back. You're not a has-been. You're a never-was.' He turned to speak to someone off to one side.

Earlston went choleric, took a step forward, became conscious of the shocked silence surrounding them, and looked quickly around the room. As his gaze travelled, others dropped their eyes.

He swung round and strode towards the door. Benedict obligingly held it open. Earlston stopped, glared at him, hissed, 'I hope you're satisfied,' and left. Benedict delicately opened his fingers, lifting his hand in the air and allowing the spring hinge to shut the door behind the retreating figure. It was a supremely contemptuous gesture.

Conversation buzzed as there was a general attempt to pretend that nothing had happened.

Benedict led Jarvis across to a group of three and introduced him as 'a lawyer who has come to learn some of the facts of life'.

Jarvis murmured something about it being interesting to look into others' cabbage patches occasionally.

'Be sure and tell us if you spot some weeds,' said Benedict, and left him.

Jarvis smiled apologetically at the group. 'I feel rather an interloper. My name is Jarvis. I'm really here on holiday, but Professor Benedict caught me just as I had decided that it was too wet to do anything this morning.'

'Ah,' said a small man in his mid-thirties. 'He can be very decisive if you aren't careful.'

'So I gather,' said Jarvis. Then he added, 'I'm afraid I have no head for names. Did he say you were Mather from Trail?'

'That's right.'

Jarvis turned to the woman. 'Pont,' she said, 'From Aberlady.'

'Lacey, from Pitstone,' said the remaining man in the group. 'Never mind,' he added. 'You'll get to know the names in another fifty years or so, when we've all got Nobel Prizes.'

'I may not be here then,' said Jarvis. 'But I'm getting you straightened out. I had breakfast with Dunne, who I think said he was from Bannerman, but had been at Trail.'

'That's right,' said Mather.

'I'll use him as the reference point till I work out the rest of the relationships,' Jarvis said.

'You must have done something pretty awful to have a morning of economics papers inflicted on you,' Pont sympathized.

'It's those sins done in secret, but punished openly,' Jarvis suggested.

Pont smiled, but apparently more as a reflex concealing confusion, so Jarvis tried again.

'I do think it's good to get to know something of what is going on in other fields of endeavour.'

'I had an uncle who used to say that,' said Mather. 'He was at the Bar, funnily enough. He used to say that a lawyer had to have a nodding acquaintanceship with all sorts of things because he would never know when some stray piece of data might be useful.'

'I think that's very sound advice.'

A voice came from the far end of the room. It was Milton. 'If you would sit down . . .'

The room was coming to order, so the group sought seats. Jarvis, to his regret, found himself on an upright, rather uncomfortable, chair. He preferred to stick his legs out and shut his eyes. For him, comfort helped concentration.

One advantage was, however, that he was seated high with respect to most others in the room, and could see almost everyone. He scanned the gathering. The feelings of the previous evening returned. How many of these were employable? Some, he thought. Dunne seemed to have his head screwed on all right, and perhaps also those he had met this morning, but Earlston was missing. Appearances could deceive, for Earlston had a fine head, but it certainly looked as though he was unstable.

Dunne, in the corner of a comfortable sofa, caught his eye and nodded. That sent Jarvis searching round the gathering for Dr Greenway. She also was absent.

Milton began to speak.

'Welcome, ladies and gentlemen,' he said. 'Welcome once more to our little gathering. It is very gratifying that so many have managed to come as usual to these delightful surroundings. Indeed, one of the questions we shall have to decide is whether we shall be able to come here in the future. If our gathering continues to grow, we shall have to think of going somewhere else, or of limiting attendance, perhaps on a first come first served basis, or by allocating of places to institutions. Perhaps you could comunicate your opinion to members of the executive.'

All over the room Jarvis saw people settling down, letting the words wash over them. The door moved, allowing someone to listen. As Milton reached a natural break, the door opened and Kate Greenway came in, somewhat flushed. Dunne waved to her, indicating there was space beside him on the sofa. She ignored him, and made her way to the back of the room, not far from Jarvis.

Milton had started to introduce the speaker for the first
session when Jarvis dragged his attention back to him. It
seemed, according to Milton, that everyone was looking
forward to the contribution which the speaker was going to
make to this most difficult of subjects. Jarvis thought the
subject would be even more difficult for himself, for he had
no idea what it was going to be. Mather, sitting beside him,
obligingly tilted a sheet of paper for him to read: 'Economic
Misjudgments.' Jarvis was not much wiser, and began to
wonder whether a drenching walk might have been a better
bargain for his morning's entertainment.

Some minutes later there was no doubt in his mind. The
speaker was Huntley, though 'speaker' was a misrepresen-
tation. Whatever his ability at repartee, his presentation of
his paper was deadly. Jarvis was not competent to judge the
ideas, but as a technical matter of communication the paper
and its delivery could be faulted on almost every ground.
And, from the viewpoint of an outsider, the jargon was
dense. Jarvis instinctively distrusted such. He had been
taught that the better you know your stuff the more simply
you can communicate it. Complexity often, though not
invariably, concealed confusion.

On the other hand, it could be that the paper was brilliant,
a fundamental statement to which historians would look as
the first exposition of some wonderful development. What
would they call it? 'The paradigmatic encapsulation of
Huntleyan economics which burst on an astonished
audience . . .' or some such fantoufle. But a glance round the
audience quelled that fancy. There were signs of restiveness
among the younger members; the more senior seemed uni-
formly to be asleep. Jarvis followed their example.

When Huntley stopped, Jarvis came awake quickly, conscious of a change in his surroundings, but it was only when
the reedy voice of Milton, and then his portly figure, rose
at the front of the lounge, that Jarvis realized the paper was
over. He looked at his watch. Fifty-five minutes. There was,

however, some compensation, for Milton, having thanked Huntley for his paper, announced that coffee was due and that therefore the question time would have to be abandoned. None the less, he felt sure that many would be pressing Mr (sorry, Doctor) Huntley during the coffee break with questions relating to his most stimulating and interesting paper.

There was a spatter of applause as Milton sat down, and then a silence before, punctually on the half-hour, the door opened and a maid wheeled in a trolley with coffee and biscuits. The captives, released, got up to stretch their legs.

Jarvis carried his coffee back to where Kate Greenway had not moved from her seat.

'Are you all right?' he asked.

'Yes,' she assured him. 'Quite all right. But something happened here this morning, didn't it?'

Jarvis briefly brought her up to date on what he had seen.

'I see,' she said pensively.

They sat in silence a moment.

'Can I get you a coffee?' Jarvis asked.

'Please. That would be lovely.'

'White?'

'Yes. One sugar, please.'

Back in the queue, Jarvis found himself behind Huntley, who had no one talking to him. It seemed a shame, so Jarvis decided to be polite as he poured Kate's coffee from the other pot.

'Complex stuff,' he observed.

'Yes indeed,' said Huntley. He leaned close to Jarvis. 'Confidentially, I am not sure that it wasn't above their heads,' he said in a voice which Jarvis could have heard at ten paces.

'Above mine,' said Jarvis, and escaped.

*

At the end of the morning sessions Benedict sought him out.

'Well,' he asked, 'are there many weeds in our garden?'

'I found that paper very interesting,' said Jarvis.

'Ah,' said Benedict. 'You lawyers. Always you say two things in one sentence. That paper?'

'I found the earlier paper rather complex,' said Jarvis, anxious not to appear to have slighted it.

Benedict sniffed. He was just going to say something, when, with exquisite timing, Huntley appeared at his elbow.

'Benedict, old man,' he said, 'I'm thinking of sending my paper to the *Journal*. Is there room in the next issue?'

Benedict turned to him. 'If I were you,' he said carefully, but with thickened accent, 'I would shred it.'

Huntley bridled. 'I beg your pardon?'

'Shred it,' repeated Benedict.

'But I have put a lot of work into that topic,' Huntley protested.

'Then shall we say that your paper would benefit from further polishing? And perhaps some research? Your arguments were refuted in the nineteen-thirties.'

Huntley spluttered. Benedict turned back to Jarvis. 'I am sorry to embarrass you,' he apologized. 'Shall we go?'

'At least I do my own research,' said Huntley.

Benedict swung back to him. 'What did you say?'

'At least I do my own research,' said Huntley, more strongly.

The room went quiet.

'What do you mean by that?' Benedict demanded.

'Hilary Bailey,' Huntley said, gaining confidence. 'She was a friend of mine, and she showed me some of her draft thesis. You were her supervisor.'

'Ah, Miss Bailey,' said Benedict. 'A sad case.'

'She was not,' said Huntley. 'You tore her draft to bits. And then when she was dead, you stole her ideas for that latest book of yours.'

'You are overwrought. She suicided because of . . .'

Benedict's voice tailed off, then resumed. 'Were you the man?'

'You destroyed her, and then pirated her thoughts,' Huntley said. 'I have proof. I have copies of her drafts.' He drew himself up to his full height. 'Good morning, Professor Benedict,' he said, and marched out of the room.

Benedict turned to Jarvis, shaking his head. 'Perhaps I was too severe with that young man. But I wonder. That girl he mentioned killed herself because someone got her pregnant and refused to marry her. She was too principled for an abortion. Upbringing, I suppose. I wonder if it was him. That would fit.'

Then he straightened up, clearly casting such problems behind him. 'Come,' he said to Jarvis. 'Come and eat with Milton and myself and tell us what you thought of this morning's papers.'

3

By the afternoon the rain had passed, and Jarvis decided that he had had enough economics to last him for quite a while.

He had booked a fishing lesson with Anderson. He had booked the whole afternoon, but two accidents truncated his efforts to a little over an hour. The first of the accidents was pleasurable. Using an Akroyd fly tied by Anderson, he hooked, played and landed his first salmon. It was a good fight, and regret ran through his pleasure as he looked at his late adversary lying on the bank after Anderson had dealt with it. There was a nobility in the clean lines of the fish, its spotted sides shading from blue on top, through speckles, down to the white of the underparts.

The second accident was distinctly unpleasurable. Shortly after his success, Jarvis took an unwary step on a tussock at the very edge of the river-bank, and found himself floundering in the water. The bed was stony, with large boulders, and Jarvis fell to his knees, losing his grip on his rod which floated off downstream. Anderson, sitting higher on the bank, was taken by surprise by the accident and came running down to help. Quickly he got Jarvis back on to dry land. After that he laughed, and so did Jarvis.

'Oh my. Oh my,' chuckled Anderson. 'Yon was a pretty sight.'

Jarvis shook his arms, which were wet up to the elbows.

'Stand you there a minute,' said Anderson. 'Till I fetch the rod.' The rod had stuck against the bank a little way away. Anderson brought it back, winding in line as he came.

'Did you think that you had no need of a fly now that you have caught a fish by it?' he demanded. 'That you could just go in and guddle with your bare hands?'

Jarvis smiled. 'Hardly.'

'It's a good lesson,' said Anderson. 'Always be careful of your feet, especially if you are wading. Some places there are holes six, eight and even twelve feet deep in them. Only last year there was a student lost in one down by the bridge at the main road.'

'Really?'

'Aye. They think he had just stepped into a hole, and then not been able to get out of his waders. They were too big for him, and he had lashed the waist. That's one theory at any rate. I think myself that it was the shock of the cold stunned him. But whatever, he was drowned.'

Jarvis shivered.

'That's why I always use the long-handled gaff,' Anderson went on. 'The Commander now, he swears by that collapsible telescopic thing. But with the pole you've got something to probe the footing as you wade. Much safer. But here am I running on, and you like to catch your death of cold. Away you and get dry.'

Jarvis shivered some more, and saw that Anderson was

right. There was nothing for it but to retreat and change.

'It seems,' he said, shrugging, 'that I should have gone to the afternoon session as well.'

'Not at all,' said Anderson. 'I don't know what those folk think they are playing at. Here they are, surrounded by good fishing, walking, and a golf course just a mile down the road. And what do they do? They sit in a stuffy parlour and listen to each other's mumbo-jumbo. It isn't as if it was interesting. Everyone of them that talks to me—and that's not every one of them—says that it was 'dull', or 'boring', or 'dreary'. They're just a pack o' sheep, wi'oot the guts to ging aff on their own.'

'Still, their conference is why they are here,' said Jarvis. 'Even so, maybe you're right. But I had better go. Will you look after the fish?'

'Aye. I'll do that. You remember to be downstairs early tonight, and stay there whiles in the vestibule for the compliments. That's a bonny fish, and it's you that caught it.'

Once changed, Jarvis set off for the lounge where everyone else seemed to be incarcerated. But, with his hand on the knob, he heard the voice of whoever it was that had the floor. Muffled by the door, it sounded awful.

'How weary, stale, flat and unprofitable seem to me all the uses of this world,' he quoted to himself. He went back up to his room and got his raincoat. There was no real assurance that the rain would not return.

He stood for some minutes in the carriage porch outside the front door, gazing across the countryside. It was beautiful. The rain had cleared the dust from the atmosphere, and everything was sparkling and clear. Rooks were cawing in the nearby elms. Down in the field in front of him a cow lowed and her calf answered. Then a pigeon started far off to his left: 'Tak' twa coo's, Davie. Tak' twa coo's, Davie. Tak'.'

'To walk or not to walk?' he asked himself. He looked at

his shoes. His good walking shoes were drying upstairs, and there had been a lot of rain.

'Not to walk,' he decided, and got into his car. Perhaps a trip to Birley might be the answer. He remembered that there was a small bookshop beside the railway station.

The shop was one of those curious shops with rooms (two of them little more than glorified cupboards) opening off a twisting main room. The walls were covered with unsafe-looking shelving. In three of the rooms a central division was made by tables and bookcases against them. Here and there were piles of books on the floor and climbing up the walls, spines outwards for stability. The girl who seemed to be in charge sat at a desk beside the door, Vivaldi playing softly as she read what looked like one of the Penguin Dostoevskis. She nodded to Jarvis as he came in.

Jarvis spent half an hour poking about. He was glad of his coat. The girl had a single bar electric heater beside her but that was the only source of heat in the place. An elderly man was moving books about in one room, and at first Jarvis wondered if he were the proprietor, but shortly afterwards he saw him paying for some purchases and leaving. The only other customer was a boy who came in briefly to look through the paperbacks on a bench beside the door.

There was some rough classification of the rooms, but within each room there was little order. In Literature there were volumes of Shakespeare and Barrie's works beside several of Andrew Lang's Fairy Books. There was Dickens by the foot, Scott by the yard, George Eliot and Hardy. He worked his way through the modern authors (a flexible classification), and on through History, Geography and Sport.

One room towards the back was filled with theology. He pivoted, scanning the shelves rather than inspecting them. It was always amazing to see how much had been published in that realm, evidence of Man's uneasiness for his future.

There was an unsteady pile in one corner. He went over to it.

The book on top had the distinctive polished red edging of a Bible. Its front cover was loose, and came adrift as he picked the volume up and put it on a vacant spot on a nearby shelf. He knelt down and worked his way through the pile, but there was nothing of interest apart from three volumes of Hasting's *Encyclopedia of Religion and Ethics*. Where could the others be? Jarvis sighed and got to his feet. Was he interested enough to search?

He picked up the red-edged book to put it back in place. As he did so he read its spine: *The Auld Lawes of Scotland, Skene. Edin. 1609.* He had a find. It was priced at £30.

After that he was too pleased with himself to do other than skim the shelves in the remaining rooms, and soon was standing at the desk at the door while the girl wrapped up his find in a sheet of dull brown paper. She was not very good at the job, and ended up by trussing it with Sellotape.

As the girl copied the cheque card number on to the back of his cheque, Jarvis saw Dr Pont go past the shop-window. When he came out of the shop she was walking briskly into the railway station.

George Appleby had always exhorted his trainees: 'Play your hunches. You are trained, and if your training has been worth anything you will get flashes, inspiration. Remember a hunch is just an IQ 200 conclusion reached by an IQ 120 mind.'

Jarvis followed her.

The station at Birley is not large. The ticket office is in the entrance passage. The entrance gives on to the platform, and there is a bookstall with the usual racks of paperbacks outside it. Beside it is the waiting-room.

Feeling somewhat theatrical, Jarvis turned up the collar of his coat, and walked slowly into the passage. Dr Pont was nowhere to be seen. A timetable was on the wall beside the ticket office. He checked it. A train from the south was due shortly.

He walked on to the platform. There was no one at the bookstall, so he turned to it and bought a newspaper. As he did so he saw movement on the other platform reflected in the glass screen at the side of the stall. Dr Pont appeared, coming down from the overhead stairs. Jarvis took his paper and went into the waiting-room.

There was a roar as the train came in. Doors banged and then there was the whistle and it set off again. Dr Pont had disappeared. Then she reappeared, walking past the waiting-room. She had a large brown paper parcel, not unlike Jarvis's own, under her arm.

4

Various members of the conference were standing outside the front door, and one or two of the hardier specimens were setting off for a late afternoon walk down to the river. Jarvis parked, took his parcel from the back seat, and came across the gravel to go into the house. He conjured wry grins by his polite question: 'Had a good session?'

Inside, Phillipson was talking to Mather, Dunne and Kate Greenway. Jarvis slipped past them and was just about to go upstairs when Phillipson called to him.

'Anderson was just telling me about your accident. I do hope you suffered no ill-effects.'

'None at all,' said Jarvis, with a laugh. 'It will teach me to watch my footing for the future. And I did get a fish before that.'

'Come and have tea and tell us about it,' said Phillipson. 'All of you. I think I could get us some sustenance in the library. You seem to have had a busy time.' Here he looked round the group.

Looking at them also, Jarvis was inclined to agree. Perhaps, he thought, they had had another paper from Huntley.

They had that look. He swithered a moment whether to take his coat and parcel upstairs, but Phillipson discerned the problem.

'Just put them there,' he said, pointing to the Victorian repository. 'They'll be all right there.'

'I'll be back in a minute,' he added, and went off.

Jarvis put his parcel beside the platter, and hung up his coat. Then he followed the others to the library, which in reality was a small sitting-room with only the alcoves beside the fireplace filled with books. It was a pleasant, snug room, much smaller than one might have expected, to the right beside the front door.

The four settled down round the fire, and Mather pulled across a coffee-table and placed it conveniently close to himself and Kate Greenway, who was sharing a sofa with him.

'Sorry,' he said. 'Our need is greater than yours. In any event—' he spoke to Jarvis—'aren't lawyers trained to balance cups of tea so that they can behave in a suitably sedate manner when visiting their elderly maiden clients? Or am I confusing your profession with that of the cloth?'

'You are indeed. There's no money nowadays in elderly spinsters.'

'You've lost me,' Kate Greenway interrupted. 'What has cloth to do with it?'

'My dear girl,' said Dunne, 'that's the old circumlocution for the holy ministry, though how it came to be so I have no idea.'

'I think it had to do with the sort of black suiting which ministers all wore in Victorian times,' Jarvis explained.

'Nothing to do with holes and cloth?' asked Kate, with a smile. The pun was duly appreciated with groans.

'You know,' Dunne observed to Mather, 'she'd be quite att active, but for that flaw.'

'You mean I flawred you again,' Kate retorted.

Despite her smile, there was an edge to her tone, so Jarvis moved the conversation on.

'How have things been?' he asked.

Kate shook her head sorrowfully. Dunne leant back with a sigh. Mather hitched himself to the edge of his chair, looked at the floor, and spoke.

'Pretty awful. We had a good paper on tax policy first, but Earlston spoiled the discussion. Maggie said something which he said he had disproved in some paper or other in some obscure journal a couple of years ago. Benedict had to call him to order.'

'I thought it was a woman speaking as I went out,' said Jarvis. 'I did consider coming in, but it really was too fine a day.'

'Good choice,' Dunne murmured.

'And then,' said Mather, taking up his tale, 'we had a rather tedious paper from Dunne here.'

Dunne smiled broadly. 'That means you didn't follow it.'

'But,' said Kate, 'the dismal torpor which Jim had induced was again dispelled by an Earlston intervention.'

'I lost the floor at that stage,' said Dunne. 'Benedict tried to squash Jack, and Huntley, of all people, came to his aid.'

'Which didn't please Earlston,' interrupted Mather. 'What was it he said?'

'He could fight his own battles,' supplied Dunne.

'That's right. So Huntley said something about there having been little evidence of that.'

'I think he was drunk,' said Kate.

'And Benedict tried to round things off. But Huntley said the point depended on "original research",' chuckled Mather.

'Which didn't please Benedict,' said Dunne.

'I'm sorry I missed all that,' Jarvis remarked. 'Still, I got a book as compensation, and a fish.'

'You missed nothing,' said Kate Greenway. 'It was all rather unpleasant.' She gave a shiver.

Before Jarvis could respond, the door opened and Phillipson came in. Mather moved up the sofa beside Kate Greenway, and Phillipson sat at the vacated end.

'Had a good day?' he asked, of no one in particular.

Dunne laughed. 'We have had an interesting afternoon,' he said. 'What are the rules of Ebony House regarding fisticuffs?'

'You academics,' said Phillipson. 'You'd be surprised were I to tell you how often that question arises. But it never happens in practice. I gather the usual habit is for there to be some quiet assassination in a learned journal instead.'

'Evisceration,' said Mather quietly. A gloom descended on the group. Jarvis was about to question it when the door again opened, and the tea arrived, borne by the cook herself.

'Tell us about your afternoon. Did I hear the Commander say something about an accident?' said Kate once they were organized.

'Well, first I caught a salmon. Then I fell in the river. And then I found a legal classic,' said Jarvis.

'In the river?' asked Dunne.

'Which was the accident?' asked Kate.

Jarvis smiled. This sort of badinage he understood. Phillipson leant forward to help himself to a cake, but the movement joggled the others on the sofa and Mather nearly lost control of his teacup.

'See,' he said to Jarvis. 'I was right. My need is greater than yours.'

Once they were settled again, Phillipson turned to Jarvis.

'Come on, then,' he said. 'Tell us about your fish. It looks a beauty. Anderson was gutting it just now, and it will be out on that plate by the time we're finished.'

'What happened with your accident?' asked Dunne.

So Jarvis explained about his mishap. There were roars of laughter as he stood up to give an impression of himself, drenched, standing in the river.

'And was that how you caught the fish?' asked Phillipson. 'You went in for it bare-handed? That won't do at all. You'll not be allowed back if you resort to strong arm methods. Fishing is a science.'

Jarvis then told of the fish. The men seemed interested, but Kate Greenway said that she thought it horrid to hook any living thing and drag it out of its element.

Phillipson demurred, arguing that the fish did not feel the hook, and that Anderson would have been quick with the priest.

'Even if that is true, which I doubt,' said Kate. 'Think of the poor thing, rushing about, being pulled by its jaw. Ugh!' She covered her face with her hands.

'Calm down,' said Dunne, with great deliberation. 'I'm quite sure that if you were to be asked, you would tuck into that fish with great relish. You like salmon. We all do. But how are you to catch them? Netting is just as cruel as a hook, if not more so. Think of the things, caught by the gills and unable to breathe. Suffocated, dragged to the bank.'

'Oh, I know, I know,' said Kate, defensively. 'And I suppose they do have a chance to get away from a hook?'

'Particularly if it's me that is fishing,' said Jarvis ruefully.

Phillipson got up. 'I am sorry,' he said, looking at his watch. 'I've got some things to do. Just leave the tray here. There's no hurry. I'll see you later.' He left.

'So there's a bookshop in the village,' said Mather, resuming the conversation. 'I didn't see it last year.'

'It's not in the village,' Jarvis explained. 'I was down in Birley.'

'Wet through?' asked Dunne.

Kate Greenway glared at him, but Jarvis did not take offence.

'We never get down to Birley,' said Mather. 'Where is it?'

'It's down by the station. If you came off the train you must have passed it.'

'We all came by car,' said Dunne. 'Where exactly is it? After this afternoon, I might just skip tomorrow's morning session. A good rake through a new bookshop would be fine.'

'Is it an old bookshop, or an old-book shop?' asked Kate.

'Just for that,' said Dunne, 'I won't take you with me.'

'You can see it from the station car park,' said Jarvis. 'And if that's full, there is a car park down at the promenade, not more than a couple of minutes' walk away.'

'You haven't told us what you found,' said Mather.

'I'll do better than that,' said Jarvis. 'I'll show you.' He got up and went to the door.

In the vestibule he crossed to the Victorian piece. His parcel was nowhere to be seen. His fish was lying on the dish, surrounded with sprigs of heather and parsley. Behind the dish, its grey metal and polished hook complementing the colour of the fish, lay Phillipson's gaff.

He went back into the library. The others looked up expectantly.

'It's gone,' he said.

'It can't be,' said Dunne, getting to his feet. 'Where did you say you left it?'

'Out on the stand,' said Jarvis.

Everyone followed him back out to the vestibule. The parcel was not there.

'What are we looking for?' Dunne asked. Jarvis gave him a description, then said, 'I'd better check my car, though I'm sure I brought it in.'

'You did have a parcel like that when you came in,' Kate Greenway confirmed.

'I know,' said Jarvis. 'That's my fish here, now. Whoever saw to the fish will probably have taken away the parcel by mistake, or for safety, when they brought the fish through. Maybe they thought it was the mail.'

'It looks gorgeous,' said Kate, looking at the fish. Dunne dug his elbow into Jarvis's ribs and winked.

'The correct word,' he said, 'is "delectable".'

'I am sure there's enough there for two,' said Jarvis.

The girl coloured. 'I didn't mean . . .'

'Nonsense,' said Jarvis. 'I'm just pulling your leg. There's enough there for all of us.' He turned to Mather and Dunne. 'Would you all join me tonight?'

'Surely,' said Mather. 'That would be very kind.'

'I'll get the wine,' said Dunne.

Jarvis half-bowed an acceptance of the offer, then turned to the girl. 'Dr Greenway?' he inquired, with a slight lift on his left eyebrow.

She looked at Dunne, who turned to inspect the picture on the wall beside him.

'All right,' she said. 'Thank you.'

'Fine,' said Jarvis. 'I'll get the seating arranged, and ask about my book. I'll see you later, then.' He went off down the passage towards the kitchen, his feet echoing on the tiles.

In the kitchen his little dinner party was swiftly arranged.

'No problem,' said the cook. 'I'll tell Sally when she comes on duty. It's just a matter of pushing a couple of tables together.'

'Good,' said Jarvis. Then, hesitantly, 'Did you put my fish through to the vestibule?'

'No, that was Anderson. Is there something wrong?'

'No. No. It's beautifully prepared. I just wondered if I could have a word with him.'

'He'll still be in the tackle room, I think. You can get to it through there.' She indicated the door into the courtyard.

Anderson was putting away gear in the tackle room.

'There you are, Mr Jarvis,' he said as Jarvis entered. 'Have you seen your fish? It looks well.'

'Yes,' said Jarvis. 'I have you to thank for that, I gather. The cook tells me that you laid it out.'

'Indeed,' said Anderson. 'I always deal with my folk's catches.'

'Well, thank you very much.'

'And what did you do with the rest of the day?' said Anderson, settling himself comfortably on a stool.

'I went into Birley and visited the bookshop beside the station.'

'Ah, that'll be Douglas's shop. He's a good man with the fly himself.'

'I didn't see the owner, but that has to do with why I am here . . . as well as to thank you, of course. I was wondering if there was a parcel on the stand when you put the fish there. I thought I left my purchase there, but it isn't there now.'

'No. No,' said Anderson slowly and reflectively. 'No. There was nothing there but the Commander's gaff.'

'Oh,' said Jarvis. 'I hope it hasn't walked. I was very pleased with it.'

'Valuable, was it?' Anderson asked shrewdly.

'Fairly.'

'Hmm,' said Anderson. 'Perhaps someone has mistaken it for their own, and it will reappear when they find out their mistake.'

'I hope so,' Jarvis said.

He made his way up the back stairs to his room, then remembered he had left his coat on the stand.

He walked along the corridor, came out on to the landing above the vestibule, and turned to come down the stairs. Benedict was putting a brown parcel down on the stand beside the fish.

He saw Jarvis, and waved a hand. 'I seem to have taken your parcel. My mistake. I was expecting something myself.'

'How did you know it was mine?' Jarvis asked as he came down the stairs.

'I opened it,' said Benedict. 'So far as I know, you are the only plausible owner for a book like that here just now. My apologies.'

'That's all right. I'm glad to get it back. It's quite rare.'

'Ah, I wondered that, given its date. But then I thought that the risk of keeping it would not be cost-effective if someone brought in the police.' He smiled broadly as he spoke. 'It is not worth millions.'

'No,' Jarvis admitted, smiling. 'Well, I'd better go. I came down to collect my coat. I think I'll have a shower before dinner.' He picked up his coat and turned for the stair.

'You shower in your coat?' Benedict inquired, shrugging. 'I will never get accustomed to this younger generation.'

Jarvis smiled again, and went upstairs. Just as he reached the top landing he saw Dr Pont come in through the front door. She gave her brown parcel to Benedict, who clutched it and set off upstairs himself. No words passed between them, so far as Jarvis could see.

5

Dinner was pleasant. Jarvis's salmon was delicious, with roast and boiled potatoes, and cauliflower and cheese sauce, all just as he had ordered it. As they sat down, Jarvis wondered what his new acquaintances might think of what he had arranged, and was prepared for them to be polite, though obviously of the opinion that his taste was not quite the thing. It was possible that they were, like others he knew, food-snobs. But it proved otherwise.

'This is something like,' said Mather as he tucked in. 'I like these things done traditionally.'

'I agree,' said Kate Greenway. 'There's too much foreign rubbish forced on you if you want to eat out.' She looked at Dunne.

'Oddly enough, I agree too,' he said. 'But, if only you had told me that some time ago, I might be heavier in the pocket-book than I am.'

She laughed. 'You were trying to impress.'

'So were you,' he replied darkly.

'Come, come,' said Mather. 'Let's not have you two

sniping at each other. Even though you morons would probably not respond to the plea that your squabbling is not very polite to your host, perhaps—especially after this afternoon—you could begin to understand that it is very boring for spectators.'

Kate chuckled. 'Sorry,' she said to Jarvis. She gave a quick look over her shoulder to where Huntley was in conversation with Lacey. Then she looked off to the left where Earlston was seated towards the end of one of the long tables. He seemed to be eating solidly, and paying no attention to anyone round him. Neither did they pay any attention to him. In fact, the two on either side of him seemed to be conducting a conversation round his bent back. She pursed her lips.

'In my experience,' said Jarvis, following her eyes, 'there is a point at which you can do no more, and it is foolish to go beyond it. It just confirms them in their misery. Some people are emotional leeches. If you aren't careful they drain you, and then pass on, unfilled, to others. Compassion can run amok and blind to the possible. Sometimes compassion isn't compassion, but guilt.'

She looked him straight in the eyes as he spoke.

He went on, 'You lose out on other things. And blight can infect through too many attempts to help, or even too much conversation or a willing ear to listen.'

'Vampires,' said Dunne. 'Pass the stake.' He mimed hammering a stake home.

Jarvis turned to him. 'Only stake a vampire when it has been proven beyond doubt to be one. Until there is then no hope, hope. But you must also do your best to protect potential victims.'

He turned back to Kate Greenway.

She put out her hand and touched his. 'Thank you.'

Dunne was about to speak, but he caught Mather's eye. 'Suppose you keep your mouth shut until you think through what Jarvis here has just said,' Mather suggested.

Dunne shook his head, but remained silent, looking down at his plate.

There was a brief period in which Jarvis thought everything was going to freeze, then Dunne raised his head again and said, with a smile, 'I thought you were a lawyer.'

Jarvis raised an eyebrow.

'Lawyers make their money out of troubles,' Dunne explained. 'Stirring, not calming.'

'Unfortunately, yes. But if we get into the matter soon enough we can sometimes help solve things before there is too much damage. That is where the real skill in lawyering lies. Helping, not trouble-shooting.'

'But you need to be able to shoot trouble in order to do the other,' said Mather quietly.

Jarvis spread his hands. 'Healing is better than burial.'

'But isn't it wrong to make money out of trouble at all?' asked Dunne.

'That from an economist!'

They all laughed, and were still laughing when the sweets arrived.

After the meal Kate Greenway announced that she wanted to look at the moon. It had been rising as she had got ready to come down, and she said it would be nice to see it from outside. So the four of them went out to the carriage porch.

The rain had passed, and, apart from one or two small clouds the sky was clear. The moon was climbing, with a ring close round it. The stars were visible as well, and the planet Jarvis had seen two nights before was high to the south-west.

'What's that?' asked Kate.

'Saturn,' Dunne said. 'Saturn, The Bringer of Old Age.'

'Trust you. I forgot you were interested in such things.'

'Not Astrology. That is what old Holst called the Saturn bit of his Planet Suite.'

She laughed. 'We used to argue about that,' she explained

to Mather and Jarvis. 'I used to make Jim mad just by reading out my horoscope from the papers.'

Dunne stood silent, rocking back and forwards on his heels, the pebbles under his feet making a grinding noise.

'Stop it,' she said, giving him a push. 'You know I can't stand that noise.'

He grinned.

'You only do it to annoy.'

Mather passed his hand wearily over his forehead. 'Why don't you two get married?' he suggested. 'Then you could quarrel conveniently at home and bystanders would not get caught in the crossfire.'

The two of them quietened down at once, and the four stood, enjoying the peace of the evening. It was just like the evening before, Jarvis thought, except the company was more congenial. He even heard the same sounds. It was a moment to take and fix in the memory, to be taken out and re-lived again and again.

'I think I fancy a walk,' he said at last. 'This is too good to miss.'

'In the dark?' Kate queried.

'It isn't too bad really with a moon like that.'

It was true. Although there were large dark patches where trees and bushes stood against the light, it did look as though walking would be possible.

'The path is pretty clear,' he added. 'I was down the drive the other night, and even under the trees it was reasonable.'

'Come on, Kate,' said Dunne. 'Let's pretend we're youngsters.'

She hit him. He got a tight grip round her waist, ostensibly to restrain her.

Mather laughed. 'Proof!' he said. Then he added to Jarvis, 'We'd better not let these two off on their own. It's too dangerous if they do have a fight.'

'We'll need sensible feet,' Jarvis informed them all. 'Those won't do.' He pointed to Kate's high heels.

'I've got flats upstairs,' she said.

'Fine,' said Jarvis. 'And I suggest something warmer on all of us. You don't want to interrupt the no doubt fascinating lectures tomorrow morning by barking coughs. Back here in seven minutes?'

'So precise?' said Kate.

'Of course. We'll allow a lee-way of thirty seconds and then set off, no matter who hasn't turned up. We'll assume that anyone absent has chickened out.

'Keep them on a tight rein,' he added to Mather.

Dunne laughed.

As Mather opened the outer main door, all four heard voices raised. Through the inner glass door, which was shut against the night air, they saw Huntley and Earlston arguing— 'squaring off' was how Jarvis described the scene to himself. But, as they appeared, Earlston caught sight of them, turned and ran up the stairs. Huntley swung round at the interruption, and himself hastily moved off down the corridor back towards the dining-room.

Kate started to move forward as if to pursue Earlston. Jarvis caught her arm, and drew her to a halt. 'Leeches,' he said.

She stopped, looked at him, then nodded. 'I'll get my shoes,' she said, and all together they went slowly up the stairs. At the top, she, Dunne and Jarvis went along to the left to their rooms. Mather's lay to the right.

About five minutes later Jarvis came out to the car park to find Mather and Dunne already there. 'I have a torch in the car,' he said.

'So have I,' said Mather.

They went and got them. Mather's was lantern style, with a red cone on top. Jarvis's was a heavy-duty rubber torch. Both gave good beams, but once they had checked them, Jarvis said, 'It's better walking in the dark unless we really need them. The eyes will soon adapt.' Mather agreed.

Two minutes later Jarvis said, 'Gentlemen?'

'Thirty seconds,' said Dunne. So they waited.

Then: 'Gentlemen?' said Jarvis.

'We can't,' said Dunne. 'She'll only be a moment more.'

Mather took Jarvis by the arm and spoke to him as, with a slight push, he started him moving.

'You seem to have had the same experience as I,' he said. 'Better to get these things right at the beginning, but if not, then as soon as possible.'

Mather glanced back over his shoulder to Dunne, who stood looking first after them, and then back to the door.

'Firm government,' he shouted back to Dunne. 'Start as you mean to go on.'

Dunne ran a few steps and caught up with them. 'All right. She'll be mad. But it's your fault.'

'Seven and a half minutes,' said Mather in a prim voice.

They went down the drive, almost to the trees, then turned off to the right, down through the rockery, and so over the little iron bridge that carried the path across the stream which lay, concealed from the house, at the base of the rockery and between it and the field.

Visibility was good, the moon giving enough light for them to see their footing, so neither torch was used. But at the bridge there was a pool of darkness because of bushes that made an arch over the path at both ends of the bridge.

As they stepped off the further end of the bridge a dark figure rose from concealment. Mather switched on his torch, catching the figure full in the face.

'Pigs,' said Dr Kate Greenway, blinking.

Mather started laughing. Jarvis chuckled. And, after a pause, Dunne joined in.

'Pigs,' she said. 'I wondered if you would wait for me.' And she joined in the laughter as well.

'Now you know,' said Mather, still chuckling.

'Will this do?' she asked Jarvis, holding up a foot. He put

on his torch. She had changed into slacks and was wearing good walking shoes.

'Excellent.'

Down at the gorge, the effect of the moonlight was magical. They stood on the upper path in the shadow cast by the branches of the trees close over their heads, and looked over a silver landscape. The moon was just high enough for its light to run down the face of the birch trees on the other slope, and not cast a shadow on them. As the leaves were stirred by a light wind, it was as if the trees were a sheet of chain mail moving as the person wearing it breathed. Only off to the left did the taller mounds of two pines and a solitary beech interrupt the smooth rippling effect.

In the gorge itself there was the same silver effect, with the dark, jagged line of the linn running through it. Here, however, the bumpiness of the conglomerate gave a marled effect in the moonlight, holes and the lee side of boulders making patches of dark amid the silver. And in any event the light did not reflect as well off the rock as it did from the birch leaves, so the whole scene in the gorge was darker than the face of the slope above it. Yet here and there, where spray rose above the darkness of the linn, there were touches of white.

'Beautiful,' said Kate Greenway. The others nodded.

They stood some time, saying nothing.

'Where did you catch the fish?' the girl asked at last.

'It was farther down, round the bend,' said Jarvis, gesturing to the left. 'There's a good pool down there. You can see it, if we had gone left at the intersection back there, but this is the more spectacular bit.'

'It certainly is,' Dunne agreed.

'Careful,' said Mather. 'There's a trace of a soul showing.'

The girl smiled, and took Dunne's arm. 'Welcome back to the human race,' she said.

'Can we go down?' asked Kate after a few further moments.

'It's not very safe,' said Jarvis. 'But we've all got decent footwear on. Come on.'

He led the way down the sloping path to the fisher's path which ran along the base of the wall at this side of the gorge. Half way down Dunne slipped, and took the feet of Mather who was in front of him. They did not fall far, however, and did not collide with either Jarvis or Kate.

'Wowch!' said Dunne, getting to his feet. 'Sorry, Pete. You make a good fender.'

'OK,' said Mather. 'I always seem to have to act as your nanny. Did you know I wrote Dunne's PhD?' he added to Jarvis.

Kate burst out laughing.

'Well, perhaps not actually wrote it. But I did read the draft.'

'True, true,' said Dunne complacently. 'You pulled out some of my obscurities, and it was good to bounce ideas off another mind.'

'That's how these things work,' Jarvis said. 'It's much better if you can talk things through, or out.'

'But I did the same for you. Be fair,' said Dunne to Mather.

'Now I was hoping you'd forgotten about that.' Mather turned to Kate Greenway. 'Fact is, Jim wrote a good chunk of mine and I wrote a chunk of his. Maybe we should swap degrees.'

'And you went off with my girlfriend,' said Dunne. He spoke to Jarvis. 'Think of it. Here was this elderly professional student—' he indicated Mather—'who is at least five years older than me, who, through helping me very slightly with my masterpiece, got the stimulus to complete his own (such as it is), and, as a fee for his so-called help, took my girlfriend as well as the best of my ideas!'

'And now,' supplied Mather, 'is a happily married man of six years' standing and with three lovely children.'

'How are the twins?' said Kate Greenway, who seemed

to think the conversation was getting away from her.

'They're fine,' Dunne answered. 'But they should have been mine.' His laugh robbed the statement of any hostility.

'Now, now,' said Mather. 'You were never the man for Edna, and she was never the girl for you.'

'No,' Dunne agreed. 'Apart from a moment of sheer pique, I must confess my main feeling was of intense relief.'

'I'll tell Edna that,' said Mather, with a chuckle. 'She'll re-call your appointment as Midge's godfather.'

'Come on,' Jarvis urged. 'Perhaps we should go back up. Are your shoes smooth-soled?' he asked Dunne.

'Yes, I'm afraid so.'

'Then we'd be better on the flat. Down there it is rather slippy going.'

They made their way back up, Dunne slipping once or twice more, before going on upstream, following the upper path. As it wound among the trees both Mather and Jarvis put on their torches. It was just as well. Jarvis had forgotten that there were a few branches sticking out into the path.

Opposite the top end of the linn, the path wound its way back to the edge of the wood. There was a spur path off to the left, to the top edge of the conglomerate where the river narrowed to set off down the linn as it left the Key Pool. They made their way down it and stood in the open, with the noise of the linn behind and to their left. In front lay the smoothness of the Key Pool reflecting the moonlit trees which overhung it and one or two stars which were bright enough to show on the moving water. Kate moved round until she could see Saturn so reflected.

Still they stood, drinking in the evening. And as they did so they heard the sound of approaching feet. Jarvis recognized the shuffling gait, the occasional click, and the weird humming. Benedict was coming up behind them.

6

Benedict came up level with where the others stood out on the spur path by the water's edge. He stayed on the main path, his black coat concealing his outline against the shadows of the trees, but his face pale in the moonlight.

'It's a fine night,' Jarvis shouted to him.

'Ah. Is that you, Dr Jarvis? Yes. It is very pleasant.'

The four came back under the trees. Benedict greeted them affably. Then he said, 'I noticed from back there—' he gestured with his stick—'that you seemed to have a torch with you.'

'Two,' said Mather, showing his.

'Ah.' Benedict continued almost apologetically, 'I was wondering if you were going to go up to the Rocks of Solitude, and if I might accompany you. It would be quite a sight in this moonlight.'

'The Rocks of Solitude?' asked Kate Greenway.

'That is the name of the upper gorge and the pools. It is not far. Have you not been up there?'

'No,' said Kate. 'And it doesn't sound very inviting.' She shivered.

'You would be better getting back if you're cold,' Dunne said to her. 'We'll let these intrepid explorers make their names by pressing on into the trackless waste.'

Jarvis was about to comment, when Mather took his elbow and whispered, 'Let 'em go. Spoilsport.' Then he said to Dunne, 'Here. Take my torch. We'll only need the one.'

He passed it over, and the two set off, back towards Ebony House.

'If you aren't back for breakfast we'll send out a search party,' Dunne threw over his shoulder.

'Would it be indiscreet to ask . . .' began Benedict, looking after the departing couple.

'Yes, Professor. It would,' said Mather.

Jarvis switched on his torch and they set off on the path upstream.

*

It was difficult going at first for Mather and Jarvis. For Benedict it was that little bit worse. In the moonlight it was not always possible to distinguish between mud and hard soil, and all three slithered while coming round and across the bridge over the stream a little way above the gorge. However, once the path had bent back to the river bank, things were much easier, and at Benedict's suggestion Jarvis dispensed with the light.

They walked slowly, Indian file, up the path, with the water quietly flowing at their side. Once, all three were startled by an equally startled duck, which rose from the side of the bank. Clearly it had not anticipated its roosting spot being invaded by clumsy humans. But swiftly the silence of the night was restored, save for the wind and the occasional rustle of leaves.

'This is the Napoleonic cut,' said Benedict as they came to that part of the track, and he took the lead, his stick now tapping against the rock.

He led them right to the vantage-point above the pot, climbed up off the path and stood there, the moon appearing to silhouette his black figure, dark against the darkness of the sky.

Benedict pointed downwards with his stick. 'There, gentlemen,' he said. 'I do not know what its name is, but that is the most striking place here, amid many striking places.'

'I thought it could be called The Pool of Time,' said Jarvis, joining him on the point. 'I was looking at it the other afternoon, and wondering what it should be called.'

Mather gingerly closed up to the other side of Benedict, and looked down. Equally gingerly he felt his way back with first one foot and then the other, and gratefully dropped back to the path.

'Sorry,' he said. 'Heights bother me at the best of time.

But that is something. I'll dream of it for ages. I'm not sure
I'm glad to have seen it.'

'The Pool of Time. I like that,' Benedict said.

Jarvis stood looking down. More than half the sides of
the pot were but shadowy suggestions, the moonlight dimly
reflecting from the walls immediately below them. The
water itself was indiscernible, reflecting nothing at all. Only
here and there could its presence be deduced as the slight
rise and fall of the water within the pot masked what had
previously been dim grey, or as dim grey appeared where
formerly there had been blackness. The water made no
sound.

Jarvis shivered.

'*Ich auch*,' said Benedict. 'It fills me with foreboding. And
yet . . .' He hesitated, seeking the right word. 'Fascination,'
he said.

Jarvis nodded, but Benedict was not looking at him. He
continued to look down. By now Mather had his back
against the rock at the other side of the path.

Benedict spoke. 'The Pool of Time. Yes. It would be a
good name.' He sighed, then continued. 'Have you read *Into
That Darkness* by Gitta Sereny?'

'No,' said Jarvis. 'What is it about?'

Benedict pointed downwards again with his stick, almost
as if he would prod the surface of the pool.

'It is about that,' he said.

Jarvis waited.

'Franz Stangl was commandant at Sobibor and then
Treblinka,' Benedict continued in a dreamy tone, but with
thickening accent. 'He was extradited from Brazil in 1967,
and was sentenced to life-imprisonment by a Düsseldorf
court in 1970.'

He paused.

'She spoke to him in prison,' he went on at last. 'She
interviewed him for seventy hours over three months, and
she had before spoken to such of his friends and family as

she could. She was well-prepared. She was not, not . . .' He paused again, and then restarted. 'She was not trying to change him, but to understand. But at the end . . . at the very end, without prompting, he recognized his guilt. "Because I was there, I share the guilt." That is what he said to her at the end.'

He paused, then again jabbed with his stick at the pot below him.

'He died within the day,' he went on. 'God took him, once he had seen his guilt. Perhaps he asked forgiveness, and that was the kindness of God, to take him from that horror.'

He sighed deeply and pointed yet again at the blackness of the pool.

'She called her book *Into That Darkness*. I advise you to read it.'

'Majdanek?' asked Jarvis.

'Majdanek,' said Benedict, with a smile, the white of his teeth stark in the moonlight.

Behind them, Mather moved, and that brought Benedict back from wherever he had been. He swung round on his good foot, waved his stick and said, 'But come. Our friend here shivers. Let us go back and have something to warm us again.'

Almost lightly, he stepped down on to the path and led the way along to the junction of the paths. There, without consulting the others, he turned sharp left, led them up to the main road, and so along to the back gate into the Ebony House grounds.

He seemed to have forgotten the presence of his companions. Despite his limp, he walked on at a pace they found uncomfortable. As he went he hummed his tuneless tune and swung his stick forwards across himself, and then behind him. Because of this neither Mather nor Jarvis attempted to overtake or to walk with him. They walked behind, in step, but without speaking to each other.

Then, at the very door of Ebony House, as they scrunched across the gravel, Benedict stopped and swung round. His action surprised the two, and they also stopped a few paces from him. He swept his stick across his body, and bowed, Germanically, from the waist.

'Your pardon, gentlemen,' he said. 'I have not been a good companion. Memories have overtaken me. You will excuse me if I go to my room?'

Without waiting for an answer, he turned and went in through the door, allowing it to shut behind him.

'Well,' said Mather, letting out a long breath. 'What did you make of that? He seemed almost human for a time, but . . .' He shook his head.

'He was in Majdanek,' said Jarvis, and added, seeing that Mather was puzzled. 'That was one of the extermination camps in East Poland.'

'Ah,' said Mather. 'That is what he was speaking about to you.'

'Yes,' said Jarvis.

Dunne and Greenway were sitting on the settee beside the fire in the library. There was a space beside them and a vacant chair. Mather sat on the settee and Jarvis in the chair. Both adopted semi-reclining positions, their feet sticking out in front of the fire.

Kate Greenway looked at Jarvis's feet, and then hit Mather.

'You two are a disgrace,' she said. 'Look at your feet!'

Mather looked at Jarvis's feet, and Jarvis looked at Mather's. Without a word, they both got up, went out to the vestibule, cleaned their shoes, came back in and resumed the same postures. Kate giggled.

'Well,' said Dunne, 'this is most suspicious. The two of you are last seen by my trustworthy fellow witness here, going off with a senior academic colleague who is not the best-liked in the profession, in the direction of a dangerous river, and you come back, without him, but with muddy feet. Muddy feet, my dear. Will you phone the police, or shall I?'

'Oh, shut up,' said Kate. 'I take it he's gone upstairs. Was it worth seeing?'

'Yes, to both the deduction from the absence, and to the question,' said Mather. 'But I'm not sure I won't dream about it.'

'He's gone upstairs,' said Jarvis.

'This one,' said Mather, pointing to Jarvis, 'and Benedict got up on to a spur off the path, above a huge dark hole with water in the bottom of it, and started spouting the most peculiar things. And they inveigled me up there too. And you know my head for heights.'

'But unfortunately,' Jarvis interrupted, 'both Professor Benedict and myself had forgotten to insure him, so we let him get back down. Next time we will arrange it better.'

Dunne laughed. 'I went up there last year. It's pretty spectacular.'

'You might have taken me tonight,' Kate complained.

'Did you really want Benedict's company as well as mine?' Dunne asked smoothly.

She punched him.

Mather sat back and winked at Jarvis.

Kate turned to Mather. 'Well,' she said. 'Tell us more about your walk in the dark with Caligula.'

'If you tell us about your walk with Romeo,' he replied.

She scowled, and looked over to Jarvis, who shrugged.

'There must have been something else.'

'Not really,' said Mather. 'I found the place rather scaring, but Caligula and Jarvis here seemed to find it stimulating. Maybe it was the adrenalin.'

'He was making sense,' said Jarvis slowly. 'There was sense in it. He was in a prison camp, you know, one of the extermination camps.'

'Which side of the fence?' asked Dunne, with a cynical edge to his voice.

'He showed me his tattoo the other night, before the conference arrived.'

'Maybe that's where he picked up his technique,' said Dunne, leaning back. 'He has savaged a lot of people over the years. Maybe he was a guard dog there.'

'It would explain a lot,' said Kate reflectively.

'If he went through all that, he might be bitter.'

'It wouldn't explain the way he demolished your friend Earlston's thesis,' said Dunne.

'That's true. He really seemed to go out of his way with Jack, to shatter him.'

'I saw Jack's thesis,' said Mather reflectively. 'It was a mess.'

'He should have resigned,' said Dunne. 'After all, Benedict was not the only examiner, and Jack's attempts to salvage something by way of articles has been pretty disastrous by all accounts.'

'What about Huntley's charges the other morning?' prompted Jarvis.

'I don't know,' said Dunne. 'The story I heard was that the girl killed herself just as Benedict said. Whether that was added to by pressures from him about her thesis, I just would not know. No one would, unless she left a note.'

'There would have been some pressures like that,' said Mather. 'By all accounts he was a demanding supervisor. And with a drop-out rate as well. But those he brought through it are really something. I examined a thesis he supervised last year. It was marvellous. I spoke privately to the candidate after the oral, and he was praising the way Benedict had kept him going. They don't all do that.'

The others nodded their recognition of the point.

'No,' said Dunne. 'Often the thanks are there on the paper, but steps are taken soon after to indicate that the thesis was successful despite, not because of, the supervisor.'

'And despite his reputation, there is always a demand to be taken on by him,' said Kate.

Dunne grunted.

'I was turned down by him,' she said.

'I didn't know that. Well, well. Weighed in the balance and found wanting.' Dunne smiled at her without malice.

'But Huntley also said that Benedict had "borrowed" the girl's ideas,' Jarvis reminded them.

'That I can't believe,' said Dunne. 'One thing the old dragon is is fair. Awful, bruising, rude, dismissive. But fair.'

'He said he had proof. That he had her thesis in draft,' said Jarvis.

'No!' said Dunne.

'Benedict was terribly angry. Do you not think Huntley had struck a raw point?'

'Am I on the witness-stand?' Dunne laughed. 'No. I think that he was grossly offended by the very suggestion, not by there being any factual basis for it.'

'Quite right too,' Mather agreed.

'And I think also that Huntley's having the thesis, if he does, may add weight to Caligula's question about him being the man,' said Dunne. 'Huntley has a reputation, you know.'

'And charm,' said Kate, with wide-eyed innocence.

'You will understand,' said Dunne to Jarvis, 'that if you are disturbed late tonight by banging sounds on a door outside, this time it will probably be me, checking to make sure Huntley is not around.'

'You owe me a fiver,' Mather reminded Jarvis.

'I don't remember that,' said Jarvis, 'but I'll buy you a drink. Anyone else?'

FIVE: FRIDAY

1

Next morning, Jarvis was wakened by the sun streaming in through his bedroom window. As usual, when not over-looked, he had slept with the curtains undrawn. He looked at his watch. It was 7.12.

He got up and looked out of the window. A figure was moving along the path at the bottom of the field. Jarvis thought it was Benedict out for his morning constitutional.

He thought about going back to bed, but the morning was attractive, so he dressed. His walking shoes, packed with yesterday's *Times,* had dried out.

Downstairs he looked at the morning's newspapers which were already on the Victorian stand. The headlines did not encourage him to investigate further.

At the door of Ebony House he debated which way to go. Down by the river, as usual? Into the woods at the back of the grounds? Along the valley? He looked at the Ordnance Survey map for the region.

There seemed to be a few interesting side roads not too far up the valley, from which he might get out on to the moors above the valley floor. It was a clear day, and he had a cagoule in the boot which would keep the breeze from his bones.

Out on the moor he walked for upwards of a mile, to a small eminence (to call it a hill would have been too high praise), and sat on top of the outcrop of rock which crowned it. To the east he could just see the sea, glittering as it reflected the sun, by now quite high in the heavens. With his binoculars he could also see the tops of the domes of the communications base and its ring aerial rising above the trees which surrounded it. To the north his view was cut off by a spur of the hill he was sitting on. To the south he could make out the line which formed the edge of the foothills as they petered out into the coastal plain. He could also see the valley through which the river flowed down towards Ebony House, and another spur from the south which, presumably, formed the obstacle through which the river had cut its spectacular gorge.

Suddenly two jet fighters passed low overhead. He had no intimation of their coming, and was startled by the onslaught of noise. Then they were away down the valley, the red of the exhausts marking their swift flight. He smiled at his own fright. He knew that mock attacks on the communications base formed part of the training programme both there and for the air force, but found a sudden sympathy with the anti-low-flying brigade.

Deliberately he took his thoughts back to the scenery, and continued to pivot round the compass. To the west the foothills rose, though Jarvis knew that there were many folds and dips before at last there was the proper start of the glens and valleys. He resolved that either that afternoon, or at least before he left, he would drive to the head of the valley road, and walk through to the loch which he knew was up there.

He looked at his watch again. 8.25! It was time to be getting back.

It was then that things became awkward. Jarvis had driven up a track and had parked on a flat, grassy patch, but his wheels began to spin as he tried to get off the grass. He reckoned he had to be careful not to bury the wheel through too much spin. That, at least, was his first thought when he heard wheel noise from the front and the car seemed to want to slew sideways. But the problem got worse, and when he got out to check what the situation really was, he found that his front nearside tyre was flat.

That was a problem. His jack was of the scissors and

screw type. Its narrow base would simply be forced into the ground by the weight of the car if he tried to raise the car on it without somehow further spreading the load.

He walked back to the road. There was a drystone wall along the side of the road, and he looked along it for a suitable stone. Something flattish on both sides was what the doctor ordered, he thought. There were a few of those, but none met the other requisite; that it should be carryable.

He was pondering the problem when Phillipson drove up in his Volvo estate, or rather down, for he came down from higher up the valley.

Phillipson stopped, and wound down his window. 'What are you doing up here? Can I give you a lift back? Otherwise you'll miss breakfast.'

Jarvis explained his problem.

Phillipson pondered for a few moments, then said, 'I know. We'll borrow some fence posts from up where I've just dumped some wire. Jump in.'

Phillipson turned the car in a nearby gate, and drove a mile or so back up the valley to a side-track. A quarter-mile down it was a wider place, obviously used for parking, where there was a pile of fence posts and three large coils of wire. Phillipson stopped.

'This is our land too,' he announced. 'Over there there's a bit of a bog.' He pointed west. The ground fell slowly away from them towards the edge of a considerable rise. Here and there was a tell-tale greenness, and the brownness of quagmire. Jarvis remembered his escapades among such terrain when he had had a holiday job grouse-beating when he was a student. Some of those places amounted to quick-sand, except that it was quick-mud.

'It's a real peat bog,' said Phillipson. 'At the lower end over there the village folk used to cut peat for the winter. That doesn't happen now. But we've lost a couple of sheep in some of the holes there. All the rain has made it much more treacherous than usual, so we're going to fence it off.'

'I suppose it gets all the run-off from that face,' said Jarvis.

'Yes, that's what does it. And there's more from further up. From here it looks as though above that face there might be another collecting area or two, but in fact the whole is really quite smooth, almost like a roof, and it all drains into Mary's Mire.'

'Into what?'

'Mary's Mire. That's what the locals call this whole area.'

'Charming name.'

'Isn't it? There are several local stories as to the name. The most prosaic is that Mary was an eccentric who lived in a cottage over there to the north, and certainly there are ruins which could have been a cottage. But the most romantic story is that Mary was a lovely young girl who died in the bog when trying to run from the attentions of an Ian, who at that time was the owner of Ebony House. It seems he watched her go under. Take your pick.'

Jarvis looked around slowly. 'Probably the woman in the cottage is nearest the truth,' he said. 'The other sounds too melodramatic to me. It would make a lovely opera, though. Puccini or Verdi, not the modern barbed wire stuff.'

Phillipson nodded agreement and pointed to the fence posts. 'Time's getting on,' he said. 'We'll take two or three of these.'

Back at Jarvis's car it was a struggle to get the fence posts and the jack into place. The car seemed to have sunk a little into the grass, but eventually they managed to raise the vehicle, and Jarvis swiftly changed the wheel.

'Thanks,' he said.

'Good.' Phillipson looked at his watch. 'I'm afraid you've missed your breakfast. Follow me down and we'll see what we can get from Cook.'

They put the fence posts back into Phillipson's car, and he led the way down the valley.

While Phillipson swept round to the courtyard, Jarvis parked in his usual place and came through the main door. A male voice was in full flow in the lounge. Rather them than me, he thought, and went down the corridor to the kitchen. He knocked at the door and went in.

Phillipson was standing, white-faced, with Anderson talking urgently to him. He turned to Jarvis.

'It seems there's been an accident,' he said. 'One of our guests has drowned. An ambulance and the police are on their way. You're sure?' he added, turning to Anderson.

'Yes,' said Anderson. 'I saw that young man from out of the water two years ago. This one has been down the linn.' He shuddered. 'I got him to the bank and ran up here and phoned when you weren't to be found.'

'Good,' said Phillipson. 'You did the right thing. But you've left him down there?'

'I couldn't carry him,' Anderson said. 'And it was better to get help quickly. Though I suppose—' his words slowed —'time doesn't matter now.'

'Who is it?' Jarvis asked.

'I don't know,' said Anderson. 'We'd better go and look.'

'You take Mr Jarvis down there,' Phillipson said to Anderson. 'I'll wait for the police. How long is it since you phoned?'

'Not very long. A few minutes. I just had changed when you arrived.'

'Where is the body?'

'Ranald's Pool.'

Jarvis looked his question. 'It's the pool just below the cataract,' Phillipson said.

As he and Anderson passed the lounge door, Jarvis heard the speaker again. Well, he thought, they would be in for a surprise.

2

Swiftly, almost running, Anderson led the way down the
drive, then off to the right past the bushes where Kate had
lurked and along the path which circled the main field.

They went down the fishers' track to the path on the
riverbank itself and then, upstream towards the linn. The
bank was awkward, with little gullies and small lumps made
by the tussocky grass. Then Anderson stopped. In front
there was a small depression amid the tussocks. In it was
a life-sized shop-window dummy modelling with careless
elegance a tweed sports jacket and brown trousers.

It was Huntley.

'I couldn't drag him higher,' said Anderson. 'It was all I
could do to get him up out of the water.'

'You did well,' said Jarvis. He moved closer. Huntley's
jacket seemed to be ripped.

'I did that,' Anderson explained. 'I tried to hook him
with my gaff. But I had to go in after him.'

Jarvis went closer. The face was bruised and battered,
the hair lank and plastered down by the water. He felt the
artery in the neck. The body was cold and inert.

'Are you a medical man?' Anderson asked.

'No.' Jarvis's thoughts were elsewhere.

'Just wondered. You seemed to know what you were
doing.'

'No,' said Jarvis again. 'No. Some things you learn, and
never forget.'

'National Service?'

'Something like that. Look. Why don't you go back and
bring the police down when they come. Mr Phillipson may
have to cope with the Conference. I'll be all right here.'

Anderson thought a moment and then agreed.

Standing beside the body, Jarvis found, as in the past, his
senses more acute in the presence of death. The air suddenly

seemed to have a tang. The crystal blue of the sky held a depth. He heard a lark, and caught sight of it spiralling above the other bank.

He looked down. The body seemed as if it were standing to attention, though lying flat. He told himself that that must be the effect of it being dragged, presumably by the shoulders, away from the edge of the river. Absently he noticed that Huntley had had on a pair of brown brogues, not unlike a favourite pair of his own, which was back in the room at Ebony House. Or that, at least, was his deduction, for only the left foot was shod. The other had on a grey sock. The water must have stripped the other shoe from the body. Or Huntley had had on odd shoes, and but one had survived the journey down the linn.

Jarvis shook his head. His habit of running optional explanations was getting out of hand. He crouched and looked at the shoe. It was almost new, the leather sole scratched but not as yet properly roughened. Was that the explanation? Either Huntley had decided not to get the shoe soled with rubber, or he had, quite properly, deferred getting it rubber-soled until the leather was sufficiently worn and scratched to make the rubber stick well. If it was frugality, it had had a fearful price. If it was a sensible decision, it had been belied. Whatever the reason, it was not—he corrected himself—it had not been, a wise choice of footwear in which to venture near the linn. The rocks were slippy. The green algæ which grew in the spray, and here and there the rotting leaves of last autumn, saw to that. Add the pitfalls and bumps of the conglomerate, and you had difficult going. Take smooth leather shoes on to that mixture, and you were asking for a fall. Take that fall too close to the edge . . .

As he rose to his feet, he saw again the face. He wondered if there was an unbroken bone behind it. It still was a face. It still was Huntley, and yet it was so bruised and battered. As he looked at it his vision swam, and briefly in his mind's eye he once more saw Patricia fall, dying, to the snow. He suppressed the vision and looked upstream to the foot of the linn, where the water swirled and surged. He walked towards it.

The water roiled to his left as he climbed carefully at the edge of the linn. Was it malevolent? Was it quite impersonal? Was it hoping that he too would slip and disappear into its maelstrom? Or could it not care less, for it could not care at all? He stopped and wondered. Why, God? Why?

Huntley had not been a pleasant individual. But had he deserved such a death? Spinning, turning, sweeping on, banging against rocks, the lungs bursting, and then the fatal breath.

Suddenly Jarvis nearly doubled over as pain hit him, and he almost lost his footing among holes and protruberances of the conglomerate. Sweat sprang. He regained his balance and cautiously took a couple of steps back to safety.

Once there he thrust his hand into his jacket pocket. His pills were not there. His ulcer had been fine for a few days, and he realized that he had left his pills sitting on the bedside table. But the lack of breakfast and the stress of the morning had set things going again. He arched himself, bending to the right, trying to ease the muscles, and massaging his side. As he did so, he noticed that the algæ on the rock seemed to have been disturbed. He could not be certain, but the marks were not quite where he himself had been standing. Had he stumbled on where Huntley had gone over? Then the irreverent part of his mind seized on the pun, and with equal swiftness his gut punished him by a twinge.

Carefully he went back to where he had been. There did seem to be marks. And was that a scrape, going over the edge into the cataract? He massaged his side, and turned slowly and carefully, following the line of the linn with his eye. As he did so he saw the ambulance men arrive, and with them, the police.

*

He arrived back at the body at the same time as they got there. One of the ambulance men leant over the body, clucking his tongue with a disapproving 'tsk, tsk'. He too felt the carotid artery, and straightened, shaking his head.

'Nothing there,' he said to a colleague. The other nodded. He was carrying a small cylinder with a transparent face-mask attached to a flexible tube. The other had a folding stretcher.

There were two policemen, one an inspector. He said, 'No point in trying?'

'None,' said the ambulance man. 'He's been gone a good while.' He bent over again, and lifted the arm.

'There just might be rigor setting in,' he said. 'The water won't have helped. It's difficult to tell with the water.'

'Right,' said the Inspector, almost, Jarvis felt, with a tone of relief. 'Go back and radio in,' he said to his colleague. 'It's a male, mid-thirties, drowned in the Lee river, just below the linn. We'll give them more when we know it.'

Jarvis spoke. 'It's Huntley. I am afraid I don't know his Christian name. He's—he was attending the conference that is going on up at Ebony House.'

'Thank you,' said the Inspector. 'Got that? Off you go.' The constable left and the inspector turned to Jarvis. 'Might I ask who you are, sir?' he asked.

'Jarvis,' said Jarvis. 'I'm staying at Ebony House—not with the conference. I came back from up the valley with Commander Phillipson, and came down here with Anderson when he told us what had happened. But he was getting cold—he'd been in the river to get the body out—so I sent him back.'

'Ah yes,' said the Inspector. 'We saw him when we arrived. He said he had left someone down here with the body. I hope you haven't touched it,' he added in a question-ing tone.

'No,' said Jarvis. 'At least, yes. Yes, I did. I checked his pulse, just like you did.' He turned to the ambulance man.

'There was nothing. And the body was quite cold.'

The ambulance man nodded.

'I walked up the linn,' said Jarvis. 'I saw he had on leather soles. I think there are marks up there where he may have fallen. At least that wasn't the order. I did notice he had on leather soles, but I walked up really just to look at the water. It was when I was up there that I saw the marks.'

'All right,' said the Inspector to the ambulance men. 'You can have him. There's no point in waiting around.' He turned back to Jarvis. 'Perhaps you could show me what you mean.'

Together they made their way upstream, Jarvis deliberately leading the policeman on the fishers' path which lay some thirty to forty feet back from the river at the base of the rise to the upper path. Once approximately level with the spot, he led the way out over the conglomerate. On the way the policeman stumbled, '*Cadit quæstio; cadit quæstor*,' murmured Jarvis, helping the man up. 'Are you all right,' he asked, instantly regretting the pun.

'Yes. Fine.' The policeman stood some moments breathing heavily. Then: 'What did you say?' he asked.

'Latin. I teach Law. The theoretical stuff. You folk do the practice. It means "The question falls"; there is no further possible argument.'

The policeman looked baffled.

'You fell. Probably Huntley fell like that too. But nearer the edge,' Jarvis said. He led the way the few steps further, and pointed. 'There.'

The Inspector looked and nodded. Then he looked again. 'There are two sets of marks,' he said. 'Or even three.'

'I took you round the safe way,' said Jarvis. 'Actually I came up by the side of the water. I slipped just about there. It gave me quite a turn. It was when I looked back that I saw the other marks.'

'Nasty.'

'Quite.'

'So you made the other marks?'

'Yes.

'Then that seems to be that. I'll just go and get a couple of stones and mark this spot. We'll need to come back here and measure things for the report, but it seems open and shut to me.'

Jarvis helped the Inspector. Together they laid one large stone, carried by the policeman, and five small pebbles, which Jarvis carried, the large stone balanced on top of another half buried in the conglomerate, and the five in a straight line running from it in the direction of the scrapes.

'Thanks.' The Inspector stood as Jarvis had done and looked down the linn and its seething stream. 'Poor sod,' he said, and sighed.

'Anderson tells me you had another last year down at the lower bridge.'

'Yes, tragic. He'd stepped into a pot.'

'That reminds me,' said Jarvis. 'You'll find that the jacket is torn.'

'I saw that.'

'Anderson told me that he tried to use the gaff at first to pull him in. It didn't work and he had to go in after him.'

'I see. Thanks. I'll need to ask Hugh about that, but it's helpful of you.'

'It's been a shock for him.'

'Yes,' said the Inspector. Then he added, 'His middle son died in a drowning accident five years back.'

'I didn't know. That makes it worse.' Jarvis nodded questioningly at the river.

'No,' said the Inspector. 'He was away on a camping holiday. I had to break it to him.' He shook his head again. 'A waste,' he said. 'A waste.'

Jarvis stood beside him, rubbing his stomach.

'Are you all right?'

'Yes,' Jarvis said. 'It's my ulcer,' he added by way of

explanation. 'This morning I had no breakfast with all this business.'

'You said you were up the valley with the Commander.'

'That's right.'

'I wonder if anyone saw the deceased coming down here.'

'I did see someone walking down this way very early on. It must have been about quarter past seven. My room looks out to the front of the house.'

'We may need to ask you about that. But it will be impossible to be anything like accurate about time of death. The chill factor of the water, you know.'

'Will you do a post-mortem?' asked Jarvis, slightly surprised.

'Oh yes. Standard procedure in case of sudden death. You never can be sure what will come up. This one, for example. You and I both think he probably slipped, just like I did. But it could have been a cerebral hæmorrhage, or a coronary.'

'But do you want to know that?'

'Afraid so,' said the Inspector. 'Still,' He added, looking carefully at Jarvis, 'I think it's time we got you back for some breakfast. You look a bit pale, and these things are always unpleasant. You'll not have seen sudden death before.'

'I am afraid I have.'

'Oh?' said the policeman, but Jarvis did not elaborate, and instead led the way back to the fishers' path, and then up to the upper path.

3

At the house, while Jarvis waited silently for him, the Inspector checked with the constable that he had put through the message, then told him to say they would not be very much longer, but that a couple of things had to be attended to.

'Now,' said the Inspector, 'perhaps we can get something for the cold.' He led the way indoors. As they went past the door to the lounge, Jarvis again heard a muffled voice holding forth.

His suspicion that the Inspector knew his way about the place was confirmed when he marched into the kitchen without knocking and boomed out, 'Annie! Annie! Where are you? There are two here that could do with something to eat.'

The cook appeared from a back room and greeted him. 'It's you, Robin. I just wondered if it would be you that they would send. It is true, then? There has been an accident?'

'Yes,' said the Inspector, unabashed by the familiar address. 'One of your guests has taken a header into the linn and drowned, I am afraid.'

'It should be fenced off. I've said that for years. It is too dangerous down there.'

'But it is beautiful,' interjected Jarvis. 'It would be a shame to spoil it with a fence.'

'I agree,' said the policeman. 'We have too much of this looking after folk, and protecting them from the consequences of their own carelessness.' He noticed Jarvis massaging his side, and remembered. 'But we are not here to argue. We could do with some food. This gentleman has had no breakfast and he is in need of something and if the pot is on, I wouldn't say no myself.'

'Gracious! Of course,' said the cook. 'That's right. Sally said there were a few not down to breakfast this morning.' She looked intently at Jarvis. 'You aren't looking well.' She frowned.

'No,' said Jarvis with a slight laugh. 'It's not what you are thinking. I don't have a hangover. I went up the valley this morning for a walk before breakfast, but had a puncture.

Commander Phillipson helped me—he happened to come along. Then when we got back here it was after breakfast was over, and Anderson had the news about Huntley.'

'That's who it is, is it?' said the cook.

'Yes,' said Jarvis. 'I'm afraid it is.'

'Well, it's a judgement.' The cook frowned as she filled the kettle.

'Come now, Annie,' the Inspector chided. 'You are always seeing judgements, and never blessings.'

The cook made no reply, but started to lay out plates and mugs for the two on the kitchen table. Then she put down one for herself as well before saying to the Inspector, 'Who have you outside?'

'Mackintosh.'

'Well, bring him in as well.'

The Inspector went to fetch his constable. Jarvis sat silent. He found that he was colder than he had realized and appreciated just sitting soaking up the warmth, while the cook bustled about buttering bread and heaping a plate with cakes.

It was an old-fashioned kitchen in many ways, with the old iron range, polished into the semblance of steel, occupying a third of one wall and giving out a comforting heat. The chairs were comfortable, with classical hooped backs. Evidently they had served many generations, for each seat had that wear which long use produces. The kitchen table was also clearly of an age with the other furniture, and there was an oak dresser against the wall behind the door into the corridor, which he had not noticed before. It had plates arranged on it, more in the style of mid-West farming America than was normal over here. The china too was traditional, platters and dishes, like the one that had borne his fish last night, willow pattern, old and comfortable too. Absently he wondered if the would-be purchaser of the Victorian stand out in the vestibule had ever been permitted to see into, let alone get into, the kitchen. These pieces were the real treasures, with the comfort of years impressed into and on them.

The cook finished her preparations and plumped herself down on a chair opposite Jarvis.

'It's a judgement,' she said again, with more force. 'He's one ripe for judgement.'

'We all are,' said Jarvis wearily.

'That's true,' said the cook, looking at him keenly, but seeing no encouragement to press on to personal matters, she took up the refrain yet again. 'It is a judgement. That man was evil.' She gave a small, curious laugh. 'You posh folk think that we don't see, but we do. We knew he was always out for the ladies, and some of them welcomed it. That Dr Pont!' She sniffed.

'Dr Pont?' exclaimed Jarvis, shocked into paying attention. Dr Pont was the very last at the conference whom he would have thought of as meriting the cook's dismissiveness.

'And upsetting that poor man.'

'What poor man?' asked Jarvis.

'The one with the foot,' said the cook. 'They've been quarrelling up these very back stairs,' she said, pointing to the door to the stairs at the rear of the building. 'It all echoes down here. It was that cripple gentleman, for he's foreign, isn't he?'

'Yes,' said Jarvis. 'But when did you hear them?'

'Last night. We all did. We were through in our sitting-room watching the film on the television, and when it was done and they had closed down—I always wait for the weather news—we came out and they were going at it hammer and tongs.'

'What about?'

The kettle boiled and the cook got up to make the tea. 'I'm not very sure,' she said over her shoulder, 'but they were arguing. It sounded as if it was over some woman or other—quite likely on Mr Huntley's part I would think, but not the foreign gentleman.'

'How do you get on with him?' asked Jarvis, but the door opened and the Inspector came back in with the constable.

'Have you been for a walk round the policies?' the cook asked with a smile.

The Inspector shook his head, but it occurred to Jarvis that the question was a good one. He had been gone for some time, more than the distance to the front door and back warranted.

The policemen settled themselves down, and the cook poured them tea in large cups. They helped themselves to buttered bread and cheese. Jarvis took his cup and cradled it in his hand, unconsciously hunching himself slightly to the right as he did so. The Inspector saw this, and scanned the pale face opposite him. Then he turned to the cook and said, 'Annie, I told you that this gentleman had had no breakfast. Bread and cheese will not do him any good. Have you nothing better than that?'

'Oh dear,' said the cook. 'So you did. What can I get you?' she asked solicitously of Jarvis. 'Would you like bacon and egg?'

The very thought made Jarvis feel worse, but he managed a smile. 'No. Thank you very much. I have an ulcer problem. Fried food just goes for it. Do you think I might have some cornflakes, or something like that?'

'Surely. Surely.' The cook bustled off, bringing back a huge packet and a large deep dish. Then she fetched a large milk jug. 'Help yourself,' she said.

The four of them sat round the table in quiet harmony. By common consent their talk avoided the reason for their being there at all. Instead the three local people chatted about events in the neighbourhood, and Jarvis was grateful for their forbearance. At length, however, a silence fell on them, and Jarvis became conscious that the others were watching him finish his tea. And, sure enough, as he did so, the Inspector turned to official matters.

'Now, Annie,' he said to the cook. 'I'm afraid I must

ask you to leave us, because there is police business to be done.'

The cook pretended to be a little put out at this, rising to her feet with a comment deprived of its edge by her indulgent smile. 'Typical of you, Robin. Take your fill and then order me out of my own kitchen.' But she went.

The Inspector turned to Jarvis. 'Now, sir, I would be grateful if you would just tell me about your morning, everything that happened, let us say, from the time that you woke, until my arrival.'

'Is all that relevant? It's just the matter of the drowning, after all.'

'It will be easier if you just run over it all,' said the Inspector.

So Jarvis told his tale, and the constable took notes.

As he came to the end, Jarvis said, 'Of course, Commander Phillipson will be able to confirm some of what I have said.'

'I will be asking him the same sort of thing when he comes back.'

'Back?'

'Back,' said the Inspector. 'I had a word with him when I was out for Ian here. The Commander has driven Hugh back to his cottage to get a proper change of clothes. And also, in my opinion, to get him away from here for just a little. I told you that Hugh Anderson has had a bad experience with rivers.'

Jarvis remembered. 'Yes, of course. It will have been a big shock, and brought back memories.'

'Unpleasant memories.' The Inspector sat silent for a moment, then pulled himself together with a sigh. 'Well,' he said. 'I think I should just have another look at where it happened. Come, Ian.' The two left the kitchen.

4

Now that he had had some food, Jarvis was beginning to feel more like himself. He poured himself yet another large cup of tea, which this time he took without sugar. Then he sat down and went over the events of the morning. He thought long about the figure he had seen across the field. Who had it been? On the basis of the other mornings, most likely it had been Benedict on his way for his morning constitutional. And if that were the case had he seen anything untoward? But if Benedict had, then presumably he would have reported it when he got back to Ebony House for his breakfast.

The same held true if it had been anyone else. Perhaps, he thought, he would ask Benedict about it. But then, perhaps that was unwise. He had been sent here to keep an eye on Benedict, and certainly something had happened here. But nothing very relevant, after all. A drowning in a cataract like that had a statistical probability. The stones were a death trap in themselves, and slippy with the recent rain. It was just unfortunate that it had been Huntley.

That started him wondering about Huntley. He seemed to be—to have been, he corrected himself—a rather unattractive individual, though not without some attraction, he wryly amended his thought. The evidence seemed to be that he had some attraction for the ladies. Even Kate Greenway had said that, though maybe she was just getting at Dunne when she had ventured that opinion.

He looked at his watch and checked it by the kitchen clock. It was a quarter to twelve. The second morning session would be almost over. He wondered whether Phillipson would be back to break the news to Milton and through him, presumably, to the other participants, and as he wondered he heard the car come into the courtyard. He got up and went over to the window. It was Phillipson.

A door opened behind him and the cook came back into the kitchen.

'They've gone, have they?' she asked, without expecting an answer. 'Well, I'll need to get on with lunch.'

'Thanks for feeding me,' said Jarvis. 'I was needing something.'

The cook swung round and inspected him. 'Yes,' she said. 'You were. You were looking like death warmed up, but you seem a lot better now.'

'I am, thank you.' He hesitated, but the maid came in before he could say anything more.

In the courtyard Phillipson was inspecting the side of his car.

He looked up at Jarvis and said, 'Some fool nearly clipped me out there. They just do not realize that motorway habits don't work here. He tried to overtake on a dual bend, and had to clip in close because there was something parked blind on the inner bend.' He shook his head as he straightened. 'I had to take Anderson home,' he said. 'He needed a change of clothes.'

'So I heard. The Inspector told me a little about Anderson and why a drowning will have upset him.'

'Yes, that was a sad business. He hides it very well, but the wound has gone deep.'

'I didn't know. I hope I didn't make things worse. I can't think what I said to him on the way down or anything. I'm just glad I sent him back up here pretty quickly.'

'Sometimes you find you say or do the right thing quite unconsciously,' said Phillipson seriously, looking Jarvis in the eyes. 'The impulse is so often right. I have found that, and I'm sure you have too,' he said, reaching out and grasping Jarvis by the shoulder.

'The Inspector asked me what had happened this morning,' said Jarvis. 'He'll be wanting to talk to you too at some point, I gather. He was very sympathetic.'

'Is he still here?'

'He's gone down to the scene again.'

'I had better go down and see him myself.'

'What about the conference? They'll be spilling out soon, and no doubt they will be curious. I saw some of them looking at the ambulance through the big window as I came back with the inspector.'

'Yes,' said Phillipson pensively. Then his face cleared. 'I wonder if I might impose that on you. You know them pretty well now, and I really ought to see the inspector.'

'Well . . .'

'Thanks.' Phillipson smiled, and turned to go back out through the courtyard arch.

Jarvis watched him go, then squared his shoulders. Think of it like a brief you have to argue, he said sternly to himself, and went back through the kitchen to the vestibule, smiling apologetically to the cook as he did so. He sat on one of the chairs at the side of the Victorian edifice, and waited. He picked up one of the papers, which were now in an untidy pile, but found his eye scanning without seeing the words. A voice was still in full flow in the lounge. His gut hurt. He got up, and went upstairs to his room for the antacids. Sucking one, he was making his way down the vestibule stairs as the lounge door opened, and the conferencers spilled out.

Here goes, he thought to himself, and plunged into the stream, fighting against it to get into the room and round to where he reckoned Milton and Benedict would be sitting. Just like a salmon in the linn, was his thought as he squeezed past a knot of people who each seemed to have found some fundamental principle of knowledge and were busily expounding it to each other, without listening to what was being said to them. But at least it's not so hot in the water, was his next thought as the combined effect of some thirty people in a fairly small space hit him.

He rounded the last group, and in front of him was the settee which formed the central portion of the front rank of the serried chairs. On it sat Professor Milton. He was alone.

5

'Where is Professor Benedict?' Jarvis began. 'I think it would be best to tell you both together. I am afraid I have bad news.'

'Bad news?' said Milton.

'I'm afraid so.' Jarvis looked round to see if he could see Benedict.

'I regret I do not precisely know where the Professor is,' said Milton. 'I saw him early this morning as he was about to go off on today's version of those morning walks of his. He said he would have to go to Birley this morning, and would miss the morning session. Presumably he will be back for the afternoon, or even back in time for lunch. It will depend on how the buses run.'

'What time was that?' asked Jarvis.

'I'm not very sure. It was in the corridor. Not long after seven, I think, but I could not be certain. I was going to the bathroom. Why? Is it important?'

'No. Not really. But perhaps we could go somewhere quiet to speak.'

Greatly puzzled, Milton heaved himself to his feet and followed Jarvis as he burrowed his way through the standing groups and out into the entrance hall. There Jarvis led the way into the Library, but found it occupied, so he turned and went back, with Milton puffing behind him, and tried the handle of Phillipson's office.

It opened, so he went in. The room was vacant. The desk was neat, with an armchair set beside it.

'Why are we in here?' asked Milton. 'This is the Commander's office.'

'I know,' said Jarvis. 'He asked me to speak to you, so I am sure he will not mind.' He stood a few moments, rocking back and forwards on his heels, wondering how best to put things.

'Well?' said Milton querulously.

'I am afraid there has been an accident,' Jarvis said. 'Huntley fell in the river.'

Milton looked horrified, and raised his hands feebly, groping in the air. Then he looked round him, almost blindly, looking for a chair to sit down in. He slumped into the armchair at the side of the desk and sat there, inert, his hands in his lap.

To his amazement, Jarvis realized that suddenly in the face of his news, Milton had become an old man. From being the large jovial individual, confident and dominant despite his reedy voice, he had become in the moment of his speaking flabby and tremulous, incapable of dealing with such matters.

'What shall we do?' he asked.

Jarvis looked around. There was no decanter or carafe in sight.

'What shall we do?' Milton said again in a toneless voice.

Jarvis looked at him closely. He had not bargained for the effect of shock.

'Wait,' he said, and quickly left the room. He went along the corridor and into the kitchen, where Annie was in the final stages of preparations for the lunch.

'I need some help,' he said brusquely. 'I have just told the senior man what has happened, and I think he's gone into some sort of shock. Do you have any whisky around?'

Annie wasted no time. She had seen the expression on Jarvis's face. She produced a key, and led the way across the corridor to the bar, opened it, went in and put a bottle and tumbler into Jarvis's hand.

'Medicinal,' she said.

'Thanks.' Jarvis hastened back to the office. Some curious glances were cast his way by those standing outside the lounge, as he went into the office with the bottle.

Inside he poured a stiff measure and gave it to Milton. Without expression, Milton took a mouthful, and sat for a few moments. Then he took another. Then after a few more moments he pulled himself together.

'Thanks,' he said. 'Thanks.' Then he said, 'I take it that there is no mistake.'

'I saw him myself.'

'You mean . . .' began Milton, half-rising and again making a groping movement with one hand.

'No, no. Not that. I went down with Anderson. He found him. The police have been, and an ambulance.'

'It was Huntley?'

'Yes.

'Tragic,' said Milton. He shook his head sorrowfully. 'But by that,' he went on, 'I don't mean a tragic loss to the profession and all that. It is just an awful way to go. His tragedy came earlier. He missed his way, just like that other one who has been causing all the bother.'

'We think he slipped,' said Jarvis. 'There are marks on the stone beside the linn.'

Milton looked at him, then raised the glass to his lips again. He drank and said, 'Maybe.'

Jarvis looked at him with some curiosity. 'What are you suggesting?'

'I'm not.' Milton looked suddenly weary again. 'I don't know what I mean. Sometimes I get a touch of second sight. Premonition. But no. Not of that. It must be this whisky talking. What are we going to do?'

'I expect the police will want to talk to everyone who saw Huntley this morning,' said Jarvis, 'so I suppose it would be best if you were to say something to them all soon. In any event they will be wondering. I saw some looking out at the ambulance when I came back up from the river.'

'Yes. That would be best,' said Milton.

'Tell you what,' said Jarvis. 'It is almost lunch-time, so I'll ring the gong, and then when folk come to the dining-room I'll ask them to go into the lounge for a brief announcement.'

'Fine,' said Milton. 'You do that.'

He was indeed brief. He regretted to have to announce that there had been an accident this morning to one of their colleagues. Mr Huntley had drowned, having, it seemed, missed his footing beside the river. The afternoon's programme would be abandoned.

Lunch was a subdued affair. Jarvis went to his table alone, preferring not to join Mather, Dunne and Greenway, though they invited him by gesture. But something made him decline, and he was grateful to the impulse when Milton came in. Benedict had not arrived, so Milton came over and asked if he could join Jarvis. It was clear that it was less of a strain on the older man to talk to someone quite outside the company of his usual colleagues. Even so, the news of the morning cast a shadow, which both were content to let remain. At one or two tables others made some effort to regain the atmosphere of pleasantry of previous meals, but in each case the attempt soon foundered. Sudden death, even of someone unpopular, solemnizes.

Milton commented on the point.

'Curious,' he said, indicating the room in general. 'He was a pain in the neck. I was glad when he left my department, and he has had rows with many here. No "rough diamond" or "heart of gold under that rough exterior" nonsense. He was not very good at his job, and I think he knew it. It seemed to make him frantic—you saw him the other morning with Benedict, and there was an argument with Earlston as well—yet we are all quietened. "Intimations of mortality", I suppose. I retire next year, and the doctor has been warning me—though even so, thanks for the whisky—and I don't suppose I have long to go.' He smiled bleakly, and Jarvis found nothing to say. 'But even these youngsters suddenly realize how close eternity is, even to them.'

'Had he any relatives?' asked Jarvis.

'A mother. He quarrelled with her years ago. But we'll need to get in touch with her.'

'The police will do that. We can tell them.'

'There might be a note in my files,' said Milton. 'I could phone and ask my secretary to check.'

'His university will have that data somewhere.'

'Ah yes,' said Milton, 'Of course.'

6

Jarvis lay on his bed, chewing an antacid, gently massaging his side and trying to decide whether the cracks on the ceiling looked more like a series of mountain ridges as seen from a yet higher peak, or the outline of stampeding dinosaurs. It had not been a good day. The bright promise of the morning had been false.

He shut his eyes, and immediately saw water passing before him. He opened his eyes and the illusion disappeared. He shut his eyes again, and again there was water. He remembered how, years before, when he had had a summer job as a student helping with the grouse-beating not very far from where he now was lying at ease, he had had a similar experience. Spend a few hours walking over heather and bog, being careful for sheer sake of self-preservation to watch where you were setting your feet, and when you go to bed you still see heather and bog going past.

He tried to tell himself that it was the same now. It was the effect of standing beside the river, trying to watch his fly drifting where the fish lay. The rippling light had imprinted on his senses, so that the scene re-ran when there was no other stimulus.

He opened his eyes and looked at the charging dinosaurs. Yes, that was what the cracks were. He shut his eyes and again saw water. He slipped towards sleep, and shuddered fully awake as he transmuted that 'slipping' into himself slipping towards the water he 'saw', and then felt its tug. He tried to think of other things, peaceful things. He invoked Paul: 'Whatsoever things are honest, whatsoever things are just, whatsoever things are pure, whatsoever things are lovely . . . think on these things—' and his racing mind shied away. He was tired, he realized. So he let the vortex take him, and it did. It took him down the linn, and down the linn, and down the linn, and then, as he had known it would, it took him to the cable car, and once more to the sight of Pat, down there on the glacier, waving, them crumpling to the snow away beneath him, and him being carried on and away by the inexorable cable.

He dozed, fitfully.

After a little he came awake again. He looked at his watch. Some twenty minutes had passed, and he was sweating. It was no use, he thought. Perhaps a walk would help. He got up and crossed to the window.

The day was as bright as before, though the sun was now past its height. There were markedly fewer cars parked than there had been, though he did not remember having heard any leave. Perhaps he had been sounder asleep than he realized.

He heard running steps off to the right, and leaned forward to see what was happening. Mather came into view. He looked up, and waved to Jarvis to come down. Then he disappeared out of sight, below and to Jarvis's left as he entered the building.

Jarvis put on his jacket, tie and shoes, and came slowly down the stairs. The door to the lounge was open. He remembered that Milton had said the afternoon session would be abandoned as a mark of respect to the dead. That also explained the gaps among the parked cars.

He looked into the lounge to see if Mather were in there. There were one or two small groups sitting together, and two men in the bow window were intent on a game of chess, but Mather was not among them.

He tried the library next, with similar lack of success, and was just wondering where to go next when Mather came out of the kitchen.

'I've been looking for the Commander,' he said, with a serious expression on his face. 'The cook says he's gone up the valley to see to some work that is being done.'

'That could be right,' said Jarvis. 'He took me to where they are doing some fencing this morning to get stakes. My car had a flat tyre and the jack was likely to bog down.'

Mather seemed wholly uninterested in the explanation, looking this way and that, round Jarvis as he spoke. Then he said, 'We've got another problem. We need to get the Commander.'

'Why?' asked Jarvis. 'What's wrong.'

'Two in one day,' said Mather bleakly. 'Benedict's in the river as well.'

'What!' exclaimed Jarvis.

Mather said, slowly and carefully, 'Benedict is in the river as well.'

Jarvis looked at him, astonished, and Mather nodded. 'That's what I said,' he said.

'Come in here.' Jarvis took Mather into the Commander's office. The whisky bottle and Milton's tumbler stood where he had left them on the desk. Jarvis sat Mather down in the armchair and perched himself on the side of the desk.

'Tell me,' he said gently.

'Might I?' said Mather, gesturing to the bottle.

Jarvis pushed the bottle nearer to Mather and lifted the tumbler and looked at it.

'This has been used,' he said.

'Doesn't matter.' Mather took a mouthful from the bottle. Jarvis waited.

'Kate, Jim and I went for a walk this afternoon,' said Mather slowly. 'The session was cancelled.'

Jarvis nodded.

'We wondered about going up the valley, or in search of your bookshop down in Birley, but Kate said that she would like to see the upper gorge. I think she felt she had been cheated a little last night.' He smiled, and continued, 'But also she did not—no, to be honest, none of us—wanted to go round past the linn.' He shook his head and took another sip from the bottle, his knuckles white round the neck.

'And I remembered the way we came back last night,' he continued. 'I was fairly sure I could find the right gap in the wood, because I thought, correctly, that it was the first gap in the estate wall.' He stopped and shuddered, then resumed.

'When we got there,' he said, 'Kate got up on that ledge, just like you and Benedict did. I wasn't going to—not after last night—but, thank God, Dunne got up there with her.

'She looked down, and screamed. Dunne grabbed her and just threw her back at me. At any rate I caught her, and Dunne too, for he came off that ledge like he had been hit by a train.

'I don't know which of them saw it first, but it was Dunne who went back up to have another look. He came back to us, and then I went up to see as well.' He took another sip. 'I had to. We had to be sure. So I went up on my hands and knees, and got down on my stomach to look over the edge.'

He looked up, and Jarvis nodded encouragingly at him. He went on, 'I'm sure it's Benedict. He's there. Going round and round in the middle of that pool.'

The two sat together, Mather bent forward looking at the carpet. Jarvis moved slightly closer and put his hand on the man's shoulder. As they were placed he could see out of the window into the courtyard. A maid passed across the window carrying a jug. Somewhere a dog barked. Then, with a swish of tyres, a police car drew into the courtyard and parked beside the door into the kitchen. Only its rear

was visible from the desk. Jarvis went across to the window
to see better.

The Inspector had returned.

7

They found Dunne and Kate Greenway sitting on a fallen
tree beside the path in from the road to the upper gorge.
She was very pale, and he was not much better. Dunne got
to his feet as they came down the track.

'That was quick,' he said.

'The Inspector arrived to make some inquiries about
Huntley just as Mather was telling me about things here,'
explained Jarvis. 'The Commander is up the valley dealing
with a fencing problem,' he added. Then he introduced the
Inspector to Dunne and Greenway.

'A bad business,' the Inspector said.

Kate Greenway shuddered, and Dunne put an arm round
her.

'Would you mind if we did not come back with you?'
asked Dunne.

'No,' said the Inspector. 'That's all right. I'll need to talk
to you later on perhaps, but . . .' He paused and then said
to the constable, 'Ian, you take the lady and gentleman back
to the house, and then come back here. We'll be down at
the river.'

The three set off back to the road, and the other three
made their way, less hastily now, down towards what was
waiting for them.

'He's in the Devil's Pot, you said?' asked the Inspector.

Mather hesitated. 'I don't know. I don't know the names.'

'It's the big pot, the main one.'

'Yes,' said Mather. 'That's it.'

At the river everything was still and silent. There was a
patch of sickness on the path. Clearly the events had been

too much for one or other. They stepped over it and together the Inspector and Jarvis made their way on to the outcrop and across to the edge. Mather, gritting his teeth, was a step in the rear.

Down in the water the body slowly rotated, not quite on its axis, the feet making the larger circle.

Everything seemed preternaturally clear to Jarvis. At one glance he took in the scene. He saw the body, the sodden raincoat, one arm extended and the other bent, both above the head, and bobbing over at the crack which was the evidence of the outlet to the pool, the walking-stick.

He sighed.

The Inspector rubbed the side of his face with his hand.

'Well now,' he said. 'This is a problem.'

Jarvis looked questioningly at him.

'How do we get him out?'

Jarvis turned and looked down again. The problem was real. They were some twenty-five to thirty feet above the body, and the walls of the pot were sheer.

'We'll need someone on the end of a rope, and another rope to get round the body to get it up,' said the Inspector.

By mutual but unspoken consent the three made their way off the outcrop, and stood leaning against it on the path. Mather began to shake.

'I wonder if you would stay here,' said the Inspector to Jarvis. 'I need to radio in for help, and Mr Mather here could be got back to the house.' He turned apologetically to Mather. 'I am sorry to have asked you to come out again.'

'It's all right,' said Mather. 'I thought it wouldn't be as bad the second time. But it is. It is,' he repeated, rubbing his hands together and then stuffing them into his jacket pockets in an attempt to stop their shake.

'I'll stay,' said Jarvis. 'He could have been a friend.'

The Inspector looked curiously at him as he said this, and then abruptly nodded. 'All right,' he said. 'I won't be long.'

He and Mather set off along the chiselled path, Mather walking close to the wall, not the river side of the path.

When they were gone from sight and sound, Jarvis once more got up on to the outcrop and stood looking down at the body. It looked frail and defenceless, almost as if it were frozen in position, its outline etched by foam. And yet oddly, Jarvis was reminded of an illustration to one of the Pooh books. If Benedict had been vertical and not horizontal, he would have looked remarkably like—was it Christopher Robin, or was it Pooh?—skipping down a track into the sunset. He shook his head.

Sounds were coming back. Jarvis was not sure whether they had been there all the time and he was just newly conscious of them, or whether they had previously been absent. Somewhere, upstream, rooks began to caw, and he saw two or three in their dipping flight above the rocks above the gorge. Mating, he thought. Mating flight. Life goes on despite tragedies.

And what, he wondered, about the life now closed, the remains of which circled endlessly below him. What would George Appleby say? And was this why he had been sent? Was something suspected down in London, so they sent someone they knew already to be on hand just in case? An impartial observer. He would not put it past them.

And yet, he thought, George knew him. He knew why he had left the service: Pat had died—by his error. George would not have sent him into this if he had really known what might happen.

And as he looked down, Jarvis saw the circling figure change. A cloud passed, and the water ceased to be dark brown, and momentarily reflected white. The circling movement took the body into such a position that it reminded him of that other figure, crumpling in the snow. He, in his turn, began to shake, turned blindly and sought the safety of the path. There he sat, his legs dangling, and looked about. So much for his protective shell, his professionalism!

The squirrels' fir tree caught the sunlight, and he got up and walked the few steps to it. As usual, there were evidences of their meal under the tree, but no sign of the animals themselves. He scanned the trees on the banks above the path, but there was no sign of movement. Either they were somewhere else, or they were quietly watching, waiting for him to go. He wished he could oblige.

He walked further down the path to where the river, having left the pot, came in sight again, and then he went the further few yards to see down the length of the river to the lower gorge and the linn.

The water there, reflecting the sky, was a deep blue, dappled with the white reflection of the few clouds that had appeared as the day wore on. The meadow on the other side of the water was a rich green, spotted with the startling red-brown of the earth where moles had thrown up their earthworks. Cows grazed, making occasional belching noises of contentment which carried clearly across the water. It was so peaceful and lovely that Jarvis felt angry. How dare things be so normal, so nice, when a body lay in the river so close by? He returned to his post.

Some time later the Inspector reappeared with his constable. He looked at Jarvis, who took it as an inquiry and shook his head. But the Inspector had other intentions, and took him by the arm.

'You're looking as bad as those others,' he said. 'But I am grateful to you for your help. Come, I'll take you back to the house too. Then I'll go up the valley to fetch the Commander. The cook tells me he'll be beside Mary's Mire.'

'That's right,' said the chilled Jarvis. 'That's where we went this morning.'

'Good,' said the Inspector. 'It will take some time for what we need to come from Birley, so that will give me time. You stay here, Ian. I'll be back shortly.'

The constable nodded and walked the few feet to the

outcrop, where he sat, as Jarvis had done, hitching himself on to the cut edge of the path.

'Don't get a chill,' said the inspector.

The constable shook his head.

'What did you call that place?' asked Jarvis as they made their way in single file along the track through the trees to the road.

'The Devil's Pot,' said the Inspector, from behind him.

'Good name,' said Jarvis. 'We were talking about its name last night, Mather, Benedict and I. None of us thought of that.'

The Inspector grunted.

'Benedict was fascinated by it, you know,' continued Jarvis. 'Almost as if he had some sort of premonition, and yet he was very cheerful. Very cheerful.'

'I'll get you to make a statement later,' said the Inspector.

Jarvis accepted the rebuke, and they continued in silence to the car.

8

At Ebony House, Jarvis found Mather with Greenway and Dunne sitting quietly in the library. The fire had been lit, and logs were crackling in the grate. There was a tray with the remains of tea and cakes on a small table beside them.

Kate looked up as Jarvis came in, and got up, saying, 'I'll get some more.' She picked up the tray and went out.

Jarvis said nothing, but pulled up a chair to join the others and sat down heavily. He stretched out his legs and sighed. Mather nodded. Dunne leaned back on the sofa, looked up at the ceiling, and then resumed staring at the fire. Jarvis and Mather followed his eyes.

The wood was mainly birch, but a fir log had recently been added, and it was smoking. Then the oils and resin caught fire, and small jets of flame began to issue from one or two of the knots. Mather leaned forward, put his hand into the fireplace, and waved out a few puffs of smoke, which filled the room with the scent of the wood. The three sat, enjoying it, each lost in his own thoughts.

When Kate came back in, she frowned at first at the smell, but Dunne looked up at her, put his finger to his lips and indicated that she should put the tray down near Jarvis. She did so, and sat down beside Dunne.

Jarvis consumed two cups of hot sweet tea and a slice of cake before anyone spoke. Then Mather said quietly, 'Last night, he knew.'

Jarvis nodded agreement.

'But he had no reason. He of all men . . .' Kate Greenway's voice trailed off.

Jarvis looked expressionlessly at Mather and said to her, 'What do you mean?'

'I could understand Huntley,' she said. 'But not Benedict.'

Dunne intervened. 'It would be ironic, wouldn't it, if they have both committed suicide. Suppose Huntley really did have something to prove that Benedict had lifted some of his ideas from that girl's thesis, and that the threat had been just too much for Benedict's pride—he was very proud, you know. It would have fitted with his Prussian ancestry.'

'Polish,' Jarvis corrected him without thinking. He was aware that Kate turned her head sharply to look at him as a result, but did not acknowledge her gaze.

'Whatever,' went on Dunne reflectively. 'And suppose that Huntley was in fact fearful of something in his past that Benedict could expose, and that Benedict threatened to do just that in that row last night? It would be ironic if they both ended it a couple of hundred yards away from each other in the same river on the same morning.'

'Very,' said Jarvis gently.

'More likely that Huntley pushed Benedict, and then killed himself,' said Mather, coming slowly back from wherever he had been.

'Or the other way round. Or someone else killed the two of them. Or Huntley was an accident and Benedict has been killed. Or Benedict had a touch of vertigo, and Huntley was killed. Or they were both accidents, or both had coronaries or cerebral hæmorrhages. Or . . .' Jarvis waved his hand in the air. Then he remembered the expansive gestures of Benedict, and brought it down to his side. He picked up his cup and looked at the tea-leaves inside.

Mather gave vent to a bark of laughter.

'Now I've seen everything. Counsel lays out all the possible options, and then looks in a tea-cup to see what the right answer is.'

'You left out little green men,' said Dunne.

'Not funny,' said Kate Greenway, and repeated it louder. 'Not funny!'

'Has anyone told Milton?' Jarvis asked.

'No,' said Dunne. 'He's gone into Birley on the bus apparently. Pont says he said he just wanted to be on his own.'

'I wonder what he'll want when he gets this news,' said Mather ironically.

'He was very badly hit when I told him about Huntley in the morning,' Jarvis said.

'I thought he looked very broken when he spoke to us,' Kate observed.

'I hate to ask this sort of question,' said Jarvis, 'but what is his medical history like? He said to me at lunch that his doctors had warned him to take care. I wouldn't want to say or do anything that would be bad for him. He really was very shaken when he understood what I was telling him.'

'Difficult to say,' Mather replied. 'I know that he was under the doctors some time ago for high blood pressure. Does that lead to heart trouble or what?'

'Can do,' said Jarvis. 'And cerebral. A shock might send the pressure up too high, and if there is a weakness . . .' He shrugged.

'Could we not get him away somewhere, or get in touch with his wife or something,' Kate suggested.

'You know her don't you?' said Dunne.

'So do you,' Kate pointed out.

'My dear,' he replied, 'I haven't been there for two years, and in any event I am not sure that Mrs Milton ever approved of me. It would be better from you, woman to woman.'

'What about Benedict?' said Jarvis.

'What about Benedict?' Mather replied.

'Who should be told?'

'No one that I know of. He's a Fellow of Palmer College, and lives in rooms there. So far as I know he has no relatives or anything. They all vanished in the War. In the camps. That seemed to have seared him, and he never married.'

'It's none of my business,' said Jarvis, 'but I do think it would be a good idea if you—' he looked at Kate Greenway —'phoned Professor Milton's wife and had a word with her about her husband's condition. Say that I was concerned how hard he took the news of the first death and that we are worried about breaking another to him.'

'I will have to say who that is, won't I?'

'Not necessarily, but I expect she'll want to know.'

'All right,' said Kate. 'Has anyone got any change? Or will I have to go upstairs for my bag?'

Mather and Dune groped into their pockets, as did Jarvis, but then he said, 'No need. We can use Phillipson's phone. I am sure he won't mind.'

'I'll need my bag in any case,' Kate said. 'I'll need to get the number from the University diary. It'll be in the list of external examiners.' She got up and left the room.

'What did you tell Pont?' asked Jarvis.

'Nothing,' said Mather. 'We thought we should tell Milton, but when we got into the vestibule Pont was there, and we asked if she had seen him. She said he had gone in to Birley.'

'This is going to be hell,' said Dunne seriously. 'It will be bad enough telling Milton and the others in due course. But have you thought about what happens when the newspapers get to hear of it? Two academics down the river on the same day at the same conference!' He spread his hands wide. 'It's going to be nasty.'

'How?' said Mather. 'We can only tell the truth.'

'And then when *The Times* and *Guardian* have run the story, the other Press will materialize. They'll get on to things you know, the quarrels, and the sleeping arrangements,' said Dunne.

'What do you mean?' asked Mather. 'There's nothing going on that needs their interference.'

Dunne laughed. 'Peter, Peter, for all that you stole my girl, you are an innocent.'

'Huntley?' Jarvis asked.

'And there is more going on than that.'

'I see what you mean. One would not want the episode with Miss Greenway and Mr Earlston and yourself the other night spread over the Press.'

'Quite,' said Dunne. 'But I think some of our colleagues are not as cautious as some others. It would be a good idea if you, Peter, were to say something about not speaking to the Press when you tell everyone what has happened.'

'Me?' said Mather, surprised.

'You,' said Dunne. 'We agree that we probably cannot ask Milton to do it. There are no other Profs here. You're the senior man.'

Mather sank back into his chair, his brow furrowed. The other two waited while he mentally ran through the list of attenders. Then he sat up.

'I suppose you're right.'

'Of course I am,' said Dunne.

Kate Greenway came back into the room.

'I'm ready,' she said to Jarvis.

'Right.' He got to his feet.

'We've just agreed that Peter will tell the hordes the news,' said Dunne. 'You can tell Nancy that.'

'You said you don't know her,' accused the girl.

Dunne smiled at her and shrugged. 'All's fair . . .' he began and stopped.

She smiled back. Jarvis coughed and intervened. 'We had better get to that phone.'

They went to the office.

Just as she dialled, a policeman was abseiling down into the pot where Benedict floated. He braced himself against the side, and using a gaff was able to draw the body towards himself.

'Down,' he shouted.

The Inspector, on his knees, leaning over the edge, looked at the rope where it ran over a bit of sacking to prevent it chafing. All was well, so he motioned with his hand and the four other policemen holding the rope let it out.

Down in the pot the dangling policeman shivered as he was dropped above his waist into the brown, cold water, and quickly he passed another rope round the body and secured it.

'Up,' he shouted, and the Inspector passed on the instruction.

The constable was soon back in safety, and the process of raising the body began. It was easily lifted to the edge of the drop, and with difficulty manœuvred over the edge to lie on its back on the outcrop.

'Well, now. Well, now,' said the Inspector slowly, looking down at it.

The eyes were open and the face was pale, but tranquil. The right side of the neck, between windpipe and muscle, had a gash torn in it.

Ian, the constable, turned and was sick.

9

While Kate was phoning Jarvis went back to the library, where the two men were sitting quietly, looking at the fire.

'That's dealt with,' said Jarvis, joining them. 'She got through with no difficulty.'

Dunne grunted, and the three of them lapsed into silence.

When Kate came back into the library she had a frown on her face.

'It's just as well we phoned,' she said. 'He does have high blood pressure and shock is not good for him. But she says he'll have to be told. Apparently he has pills, and we are to make sure he doesn't drink.'

'Oh!' said Jarvis. 'I got him whisky this morning.'

'He does drink quite a bit when he is at conferences,' said Kate. 'But we'd better watch it. Aren't there some of these pills that don't mix with drink?'

'Yes,' said Jarvis. 'It can be bad. We'd better take care.'

'It's Plan Three, I suppose,' said Dunne.

Mather smiled. 'Still playing soldiers?'

Dunne smiled back. 'Defence mechanism.'

'I think,' said Mather carefully, his face turned now towards the fire, 'that this new news should be broken by the same bearer as before.'

There was a silence. No one looked at Jarvis.

He thought, and then, to their surprise, agreed.

'You're probably right.'

The others let out their breath together, and Jarvis realized that there had been doubt in their minds.

'Am I right that you two worked that out?' he asked the two men.

'Yes,' said Dunne. 'It was my idea, if you want a scapegoat.'

'You are confused,' said Jarvis. 'I'm the scapegoat, if anyone.'

'At least, we've given up the practice of executing the bearer of bad tidings,' Mather said.

'I'll talk to Milton alone,' Jarvis suggested. 'In the office again would be best. That is, if Phillipson is not back. And we'll have to tell him too, won't we?'

'Yes, there's him as well.'

'No, there isn't,' Jarvis remembered. 'The Inspector said he would go up the valley and tell him once he had organized getting the body out of the water.'

'So the Commander will be coming back in as well,' said Dunne. 'We'll have to get to him before he can speak to Milton.'

'I'll need to catch Milton just when he comes back,' Jarvis said. 'Perhaps you could find out when the buses run, if that was how he went, and also keep an eye open for Phillipson and get his permission to use his office. In the meantime I'd like to go up to my room, if you don't mind.'

'Good idea,' Kate agreed. 'I think I'll go up too.'

But while Kate was making her phone call it had occurred to Jarvis that he had better report what had happened, so when they left the library he excused himself, saying he ought to make another call, and went back into the office.

He left a brief message with the duty officer and then went upstairs to his room. Events were speeding on, and he wanted time on his own. It was beautiful outside, and briefly he considered going for a walk, but every direction held distractions. The river would be close to the south. On the valley road there was the likelihood of meeting police cars. Even going down the drive he was likely to meet members of the conference, and he did not want to do that just yet.

He chewed an antacid while looking out of his bedroom window. Movement caught his attention so he got out his binoculars. Yes, there were some figures down there towards the linn. Ghouls, he thought, but then realized that there was a natural curiosity at work. He panned to the right and saw the unmistakable blue of a policeman clearly barring the route upstream to another couple of conferencers. It was as well the inspector had thought of that. He himself had

not realized that there might be people wanting to walk up
the river that afternoon, yet the weather was still glorious,
though the cloud was increasing.

He took off his shoes and jacket and lay on his bed
reviewing matters.

Whatever had happened, it seemed strange. As Dunne
had said, two in the river in the same day—the same
morning, indeed—did seem too much of a good thing. What
would London make of it? Had there been some hint? Would
Benedict prove to have been eliminated, for reasons he knew
nothing of? If that were so, he wondered who would have
done it, and if it had been 'home base' whom they would
have sent. He had met in all his time on staff only two who
were rumoured to take care of such matters. He had seen
neither recently. And in any event there was Huntley to
explain.

He chewed things over more and more idly, and suddenly
found himself more interested in the patterns on the ceiling.

Yes, they were dinosaurs up there, he decided. He shivered slightly, and got under the quilt. It was comfortable
and, after a few minutes, warm.

He dozed.

He came awake to a repeated knock at the door. Tousle-
headed, he got up and went and opened it. Dunne was
outside.

'He's back,' he said. 'He got a lift from Lacey. We've got
him in the library.'

'Is Phillipson back?'

'Yes, he's on the phone. It just worked out like that, with
Milton coming back earlier than we expected. Now he's in
the library it would be odd to wheel him through to the
office. It would be sure to give him some indication that
there is something bad coming up.'

'I suppose you are right. Very well. And what about
Phillipson. What did he say?'

'Very little. He just bustled in. Mather and I were in the vestibule, waiting, and he came along the corridor and was into his office before we could catch him. We went in and said that we had arranged how to tell Milton, and he said he was grateful for the help and that he had phoning to do. So we didn't raise the question of using the office. We hoped he might leave it again. But just as we came out, Milton was coming in.' They went downstairs together.

Milton did not look good. There was a greyish tinge to his cheeks.

As soon as Jarvis followed Dunne into the library, his heart sank. It seemed terrible to have to tell this shrunken man more bad news, but Milton made it easier for him. He seemed to have picked up some indication, perhaps from Mather's manner.

As Jarvis appeared, Milton said to Mather and Dunne, 'All right, you two, you can go. The bearer of ill-news is here.'

As Dunne and Mather left, Milton held out his hands to Jarvis and said, 'Sorry about that, but you are, aren't you? Once more.'

'You said something about second sight, or hunches,' Jarvis reminded him.

Milton heaved a sigh, then indicated the sofa beside the dying fire.

'I am very sorry . . .' began Jarvis, but Milton cut him off.

'Who?' he demanded.

Jarvis stared at him.

'Huntley was not my . . . my feeling,' said Milton carefully.

Jarvis lifted an eyebrow.

'Benedict?' The voice was quiet.

Jarvis nodded.

Milton let out his breath in a long exhalation, and then remained, apparently without breathing, for so long that

Jarvis began to worry. Then Milton took a deep breath. He got up and went over to stand, his outstretched hands on the mantelpiece, his head bent between his arms, looking down at the fire.

'Where?' he asked.

'The Inspector called it the Devil's Pot.'

There was a long pause.

'Do you know Dylan Thomas?' said Milton at last.

'Do not go gently . . . ?'

'Yes.'

A log collapsed with a phuff of ash. It was loud amid the silence of the room.

'I think he had some premonition himself,' said Jarvis at last. 'We were at the spot, Benedict, Mather and I, last night. We were debating what the name of the place should be. I thought "the Pool of Time", which Benedict seemed to like a lot. He himself said some strange things, but he was almost exultant.'

'Yes,' said Milton, addressing the fire. 'Exultant. That is the right word. He came in to see me last night. He had just been out. He didn't say he had had company. But I had the feeling that some deep question had been resolved. That here was someone who had made his peace with his God, and was ready to depart. I didn't know what to say to him. It was a strangely vibrant peace that he had in him, if you see what I mean.'

He paused, and continued quietly, 'I was envious.' Then his hand went to his waistcoat, and he turned to face Jarvis, pulling out a small silver pill box. He took out a pill and put it under his tongue.

'Don't worry,' he said, seeing the look of concern on the other man's face. 'This will do better than whisky, though I prefer the whisky. But my doctor recommends this.' He tapped the pocket where he had replaced the box.

'Now,' he said. 'We had better have another meeting. so that I can tell everyone.'

Jarvis shook his head admiringly.

'We had thought that someone else could do that job.'

'We?'

'Mather, Dunne, Greenway and myself. We are the only ones who know, apart from the Commander. It was those three who found him, and we had thought that perhaps . . . perhaps you would prefer someone else to take on that task.'

'You thought I would go into shock,' said Milton, with a twinkle in his eye.

Jarvis tried to demur, and then sought refuge.

'Perhaps I should get the others,' he said, and made for the door.

Milton sat down on the sofa.

Jarvis went out into the vestibule, bumping into Dunne who was close to the door. Mather was standing in the middle of the hall, talking quietly to Kate Greenway. They looked round anxiously as Jarvis came out. He shut the door behind him, and said, 'He's taken it very well. So much so that Plan Three had better be revised. Come on in, and we shall see.'

But when they re-entered the library there had been a change. Milton had slumped into his seat. The grey tinge had not lifted, Jarvis realized, as he greeted them with a tired smile.

'Perhaps your idea is the better one,' he said.

10

So it was Mather who had to break the news of Benedict's death to those of the conference who came down when the gong was sounded for dinner. As he was doing so Jarvis went into the office to have a word with Phillipson.

'I came here for a quiet break,' he said.

'Did you?' Phillipson laughed bitterly. 'I dare say I should have expected somebody would fall in the linn some day, but two in one day? I ask you!'

'It's certainly not a good recommendation.' In an attempt at humour Jarvis added, 'Still, I dare say that's your statistical probability met for the next fifty years.'

'Thanks very much,' said Phillipson tightly. Then he relaxed. 'Yes. You may be right. I hope you are right.'

'I am sure I am. You'll see. It won't take too long to deal with the formalities, and then you can get back to your fishing. You'll find it will make no difference to bookings. In fact it might even help.'

Phillipson nodded. 'I suppose that is true. I hope it doesn't make a difference to bookings in a bad sense. We have a good occupancy rate, but there are limits to what we can stand.'

'You'll see,' Jarvis promised. 'I probably won't be able to get in next year.'

'Make your booking now,' suggested Phillipson. Then he went on, 'You mentioned the fishing. You haven't seen my gaff, have you? It seems to have gone missing.'

'No, I haven't. You wouldn't have left it somewhere in all the excitement? In your car?'

'Perhaps,' said Phillipson. 'I'll look.'

Just then they heard a car entering the courtyard, and then another. Through the window they saw two police cars parking. The Inspector and a constable were in one. The other had men in ordinary suits.

'Odd,' said Phillipson. 'I'd better see what this is.'

Jarvis waited in the vestibule. He looked at the Victorian coat-stand. The gaff was not in evidence. Very shortly thereafter four men, two uniformed policemen, and Phillipson went into the office, without acknowledging his presence, and shut the door.

He stood, studying the Ordnance Survey map of the area. He traced the river, and the path from the upper to the lower gorge. The pools were not named. Then, on impulse he went into the dining-room and asked the maid to add his place to the table which Mather and company would occupy. She did so, and he sat there, waiting while the second announcement was made in the lounge.

Kate was pleased to see him.

'Mather did it very well,' she said as she sat down.

'How is Milton?' Jarvis asked.

'He's all right. He's sleeping. I looked in to his room before I came down, and he was asleep.'

Dunne arrived.

'Well,' he said, as he took his place at the table, 'what's up? The Commander caught Bill as we were coming through, and took him into the office. I'm not sure, but I think I saw the police in there.'

'You did,' said Jarvis. The others looked concerned. 'I don't know why they're here,' Jarvis continued. 'They arrived while I was talking to Phillipson and you were having your meeting. They went straight in with him. I came on in here.'

'Oh dear,' said Kate. 'I do hope there's not something else wrong now.'

'It is curious,' said Jarvis.

Mary, the second maid, came for their orders. Deciding was a problem. Rainbow trout, roast lamb, and duck were the main options. The trout was rejected on the basis of the previous night's salmon. Kate professed a dislike of duck, so she took the lamb. Dunne and Jarvis settled for the duck.

'I'll come back for the other gentleman's order,' said Mary.

'I suppose,' said Kate, 'that there'll be the coroner's inquest to be dealt with. They'll be here about that.'

Dunne agreed.

'No,' said Jarvis. 'We don't have coroners up here.'

'What do you have, then?' asked Dunne.

'In a suspicious death, where there is a question of a preventable accident, or something like that, it is possible there would be a Fatal Accident Inquiry,' explained Jarvis.

'But other cases go to the Procurator Fiscal, and if necessary to Crown Office in Edinburgh.'

'That's right,' said Kate. 'I was reading something about that. Your what's-its prosecute and deal with a lot of such things. Something similar has been introduced in England.'

'Procurators fiscal, we call them,' said Jarvis.

'Sounds faintly unpleasant . . . or immoral,' said Dunne.

Just then the door to the dining-room opened and Mather came in. He walked past the table with Jarvis and the others and stood under the landscape beside the fireplace. He picked up a glass from the side-table, and, holding it by its base, pinged it two or three times. The room fell quiet. He spoke into a silence which had gone curiously tense.

'Ladies and gentlemen. Forgive me. I have serious news. The police wish to interview everyone about both the deaths, Huntley's and the one I just spoke to you about. They wish to begin immediately after dinner. I—' he attempted a smile and failed—'I have persuaded them that you should be allowed to have your meal first. There are two sets of interviewers. One will be in the office, by permission of the Commander. The other will be in the library. They ask that you hold yourselves available for interview, and it is suggested that you await your turn, either in the lounge or in your rooms. They will, if necessary, continue tomorrow morning.'

There was a buzz of surprise at this.

Mather continued: 'They know that the conference was scheduled to break up tomorrow morning, and that one or two were intending to leave earlier. If these would have a word with the Inspector, who will be out in the vestibule, they will try to see anyone who has to leave early, tonight. If those who don't need to go could stay on, it would be appreciated. I gather that in fact there is no other conference due in here until next Wednesday. Individual bookings have been cancelled. So it would be appreciated if those who can, would stay on here for another night or so, so that this can be dealt with. I am told by the Commander that it will not cost any extra.' He paused, and added, 'I hope it does not take that long. Thank you for your attention.'

He came and sat down with Dunne and the others. A buzz of conversation began, which none the less seemed to stabilize as everyone speculated in lowered tones what the announcement might mean.

'Come on,' said Dunne to Mather. 'That won't do. What is going on?'

'It will do,' said Mather. 'It will have to.' He looked up as a maid came to the table, and very obviously gave the whole of his attention to the menu.

Conversation in the room during the meal was, to say the least, difficult. There was a strained silence which gave way to low murmurs as various topics were nibbled at and abandoned. Dunne tried to lift spirits at his table by a joke. Kate frowned at him.

'What's wrong with you?' he asked.

'You,' she replied.

'What have I done?'

'Two of your colleagues have drowned in one day, and you're telling jokes.'

Jarvis intervened. 'That's his defence mechanism.'

Dunne looked at him from under his brows, then sighed. 'I'm sorry,' he said to Kate. 'It is either that or cry.'

'I didn't ever think of you crying,' she said tightly.

'My namesake got it right,' he said. 'Never send to know for whom the bell tolls . . .'

There was another silence, but this one healthy.

At length during the sweet course Mather leaned forward conspiratorially. The other heads came forward too, and he spoke in a low voice.

'It's serious,' he said. 'It sounds as if they are investigating a murder.'

'*A* murder?' inquired Jarvis softly.

Mather looked at him strangely.

'They want to see you first,' he said.

'We've all carefully stepped round the question,' Kate said to Jarvis, 'but you know these things. Are we barred from discussing what has happened before we see the police?'

'Not barred,' he said. 'They have not asked us not to talk. But I dare say it would be better if we did not. Putting together a picture in a matter like this is like doing a jigsaw or a mosaic. Many folk have the same pieces, but some have additional bits, and some have nothing at all. It is better not to discuss lest those with the extra bits forget their individual pieces, and they get lost amid some common "explanation" of what has gone on. The danger is that there comes to be a common history of what went on, while everyone in fact saw everything differently. The police don't want that individuality ironed out. They don't want possibly to lose something significant.'

'I think you mean by that that we shouldn't talk to each other about it,' she said, with a slight frown.

He smiled.

'Will it be awful?' she said.

'No. Just tell them everything you remember, and don't put in what you didn't see or hear.'

She shivered.

'I expect it will be painless,' he said, as he got up. 'I'll skip coffee.' He turned to Mather. 'Me first, you said?'

Mather nodded.

The room went quiet once more as Jarvis made his way among the tables to the door.

He heard conversation resume vigorously as he closed it behind him.

11

The constable who had been with the Inspector earlier in the day was seated behind a small table in the vestibule set opposite the fire which was blazing cheerfully. Behind him was the stand, and he had put his helmet on the shelf. He looked up as Jarvis appeared, and then looked down at a two-column list on a sheet of paper in front of him.

'Dr Mather tells me that you would like to see me first,' said Jarvis.

'Yes, sir,' replied the constable. 'That's quite right. Just a moment please.' He got up and went over to the door to the office, knocked and went in, closing the door behind him.

After a few moments he came out again together with the Inspector, who held the door open, and said, 'Superintendent Mason will see you now, if it is quite convenient.'

The office was neat, as ever. A man stood, silhouetted against the dying light in the window. The main light was not on, but the lights to the side of the fireplace were on, Jarvis noticed, and there was one on the table, which clearly would illuminate anyone sitting in the chair which had been drawn up in front of it, while leaving the chair behind the desk in shade. There was an A4 notepad on the desk, with a green pencil beside it. Behind the desk sat a man in a neat dark grey suit with a lighter stripe in it. His hair was grizzled and starting to recede. He got up and leaned forward with his hand outstretched. As he came into the light from the lamp on the desk Jarvis saw that he had a scar and indentation above his right eye, distorting the brow, and giving him a decidedly satanic look.

'Please take a chair,' the man said, indicating the chair in front of the desk.

For a moment Jarvis considered taking one of the chairs beside the fire, but he decided not to be provocative. The figure by the window came and sat behind in one of the chairs beside the fire. Jarvis glanced over his shoulder and saw him taking a notebook out of his pocket.

The man settled himself behind the desk.

'This is a sorry business,' he said.

Jarvis nodded.

'We are here to make some official inquiries into both these tragedies, and, because you have already spoken with Inspector Paget, I thought it would be useful to speak to you first.'

'Certainly,' said Jarvis. 'Any help I can give, I will.'

The Superintendent's lips twitched. 'Perhaps it would be easiest if you were simply to go over the events of this morning.'

Jarvis did so. So far as he could remember he told the same story. In response to a question, however, he remembered that he could give a time fix for when he was up on the moor, and added the episode of the passing jets.

'I don't know if you can get some timing from the RAF on that.'

The Superintendent himself took a note of the point on the notepad in front of him. As he did so, Jarvis reflected, 'Though I suppose that would not prove where I was exactly when I heard the noise. I expect it was heard all down the valley.'

The Superintendent sat back and steepled his fingers, resting his chin on their points.

'Now why,' he asked mildly, 'would you consider it necessary to establish exactly where you were?'

'Training, I suppose,' said Jarvis after a slight hesitation. 'I am a lawyer, and I read quite a lot of detective fiction.'

The Superintendent smiled, but, although it might have been a trick of the shadowing, the smile did not seem to reach his eyes.

'Go on,' he said.

Jarvis did.

'Now. About this later occurrence?' the Superintendent prompted. 'Suppose you tell me first about this walk of yours last night.'

Jarvis went through the details of that, and then the happenings of the afternoon, the Superintendent nodding encouragingly now and again, and occasionally prompting or asking a question by way of explication. By the end Jarvis was feeling very drained.

When he had finished, the Superintendent got up and went across to the window, looking out into the courtyard, now darkened except for where lights from the dining-room or upstairs rooms cast pools of light.

'You have been very helpful.'

'May I go?' asked Jarvis.

'You do not seem very surprised that a senior police officer should be dealing with a simple matter like this.'

Jarvis said nothing.

The Superintendent turned and came back into the light, leaning on his hands across the desk.

'Why are you here?' he asked mildly.

'I came for a few days' holiday,' said Jarvis. 'I was here last year, and thought I could do with a few days off and some more fishing practice with the fly. The Commander had a gap in the booking.'

'You're fly,' said the Superintendent, straightening up. He gestured to his colleague who had been sitting silent, taking notes all the time. 'Tell him, Tom,' he said irritably, turning back to the window.

Jarvis twisted in his seat to look at the man beside the fire. He closed his notebook, and put it deliberately into his jacket pocket before speaking.

'We have had a phone call,' he said.

Jarvis raised an eyebrow, but said nothing.

'A phone call from London,' went on the other detective. 'We gather that while you may well be here for a holiday as you have said, you may also be carrying out a commission, as it were.'

Jarvis cocked his head on one side, and remained silent.

The Superintendent gave a bark of laughter. He had turned silently to watch Jarvis. 'I am informed that if you show a disinclination to accept the genuineness of what has been said to you, I am to tell you that the orchard needs many helpers to gather all the ripe apples.' He snorted again.

Jarvis nodded, a slow smile creeping across his face. That indeed was the code which George Appleby had given. He was prone to pun on his name.

He spread his hands. 'Even so,' he said, 'I can tell you nothing.'

'I know. I know,' said the Superintendent, once more somewhat irritable. 'It is always like that. But it means two things. First, that you know I know. And second, it means that I can tell you things. And there are ways surely in which you would not let us go off down a track you knew to be wrong?'

He came round the desk and looked closely at Jarvis.

'No promises,' said Jarvis.

'Well, well,' said the Superintendent. 'It also means, you understand, that you remain a suspect.'

'A suspect?'

The Superintendent ignored the interruption. 'It would be an interesting twist if you were here to do a job which has now been done, and that message to us was designed to get you out safely. That,' he emphasized by pointing his finger at Jarvis, 'would not work. If you are guilty, I will prove it.'

Jarvis demurred. 'I will grant your hypothesis, but only for the purpose of argument, and point out that if it were to be decided that either Huntley or Benedict were to be eliminated, that would not be the decision of our authorities. We don't work like that.' He smiled. 'And even if we did, it would be done by a special unit, not by someone on other duties.'

'"We"? What if you are surveillance?' said the Superintendent. 'Making sure that all goes well?'

'Not me!' said Jarvis forcefully.

'But not impossible?'

'No comment.'

The Superintendent visibly relaxed himself. He waved to his colleague. 'All right. Let's proceed on that basis.'

Jarvis turned to the other man. 'What else were you going to tell me?' he asked.

'The Professor had a gash in his throat, cutting the carotid artery,' said the other. 'The one early this morning has had his post-mortem. He was in good physical shape, but had not drowned. Our tame ghoul—'

The Superintendent interrupted. 'Tom!' he said. 'You will use proper forms of address at all times, and particularly before civilians.' Then he spoiled the effect by a chuckle, and waved his hand.

'Our forensic pathologist,' resumed the other, also smiling, 'considers that Mr Huntley had ceased breathing before entering the water. His coronary arteries were in good shape.'

'Brain?' asked Jarvis, intent.

'No cerebral occlusions, and probably no subdural or sub-arachnoid hæmorrhages though it is difficult to tell. He would seem to have gone down the linn from where you and the inspector saw the marks, and if that is the case, he would have had quite a pounding on the way. There are skull fractures sufficient to cause death, but no significant water in the lungs.'

Jarvis sighed.

'In short,' said the Superintendent, 'both men may have met violent ends. The Professor's wound looks impossible to self-inflict. There is doubt about the other.'

'I see why you are here,' said Jarvis.

The Superintendent looked at his watch.

'I'll let you go now,' he said. 'Thank you for your help. Any further help will be gratefully received.'

'Though I am still a suspect,' smiled Jarvis.

The Superintendent bowed. His colleague went to the door and opened it.

'Thanks,' he said.

12

Jarvis debated whether to go back to the lounge or whether just to call it a day and go up to his room to think over what had happened and what had been said. But as he stood, irresolute, in the hall, the office door opened and the second detective came out. He spoke briefly to the constable, who went into the lounge and came out accompanied by Mather.

As he passed, Mather said, 'They're all in there. Why don't you join them?'

Jarvis looked his question to the detective, who nodded his head slightly, so Jarvis went into the lounge.

As he came in, heads turned and a silence fell.

Kate Greenway signalled to him from the bow window. She and Dunne were parked over there, and there was a low empty chair beside them. Clearly that was where Mather had been when summoned. It was a long way across under the silent gaze of all present, as if the room expanded to make the distance from door to chair much farther than it looked.

Jarvis dropped into the chair, his back to the door. It was farther down to the seat than he had expected, and he found himself sitting with his knees uncomfortably high until he slouched back into a semi-prone position.

'This sort of thing keeps the osteopaths in business,' he said with a grin, and tapping the arm of the chair.

'How was it?' asked Dunne.

'What did they want to know?' asked Kate.

Jarvis waved his hand, as if he were royalty greeting a pavement-full of well-wishers from a state coach. 'They just trundled me through the happenings so far as I was involved,' he said.

'That's what you said,' said Kate depressedly. She mimicked his earlier tone. 'It will be a matter of us all telling our stories, and them being put together, and presumably the—what did you call them?—the "significant" bits being worked out. And then they will work on those. No doubt work on the people too, I should imagine.' She shook her head.

Jarvis heaved himself forward.

'Look,' he said quietly. 'They have a job to do, and we can help them do it efficiently. But there is no point in letting it get you down. There's nothing to worry about.'

'He doesn't think so,' Dunne interjected, cocking a thumb in the direction of the back wall. Jarvis followed the indication. There, hunched in a chair, with a tumbler in his hand, was Jack Earlston.

'Can't we do something about him?' asked Jarvis, feeling surprised that Kate had apparently done nothing.

'No,' she said. 'Not when he has drink. He'll be all right tomorrow, but now he is better just left.'

Jarvis, looking across at the sorry figure, was inclined to disagree, but his companions did know the situation better than he did.

'It's true,' said Dunne. 'He is an obnoxious, paranoid basket when he is sober. But he has been back twice to the bar. That is his third. History indicates that he will shortly go off to his pit. And all will be well in the morning. But if you try to say anything to him just now there would be an explosion. He is quite unpredictable when he is in this state. I mean, there would be an explosion, but whether it would be directed at you, or at some other of the phantoms he so carefully nurses, could not be predicted. I think he'll be all right if left alone. So long as he doesn't think someone else is in Kate's room . . .' His voice trailed off. He got up and went across to her, where, soundlessly she was crying as she sat. Her face was expressionless, not a 'crying' face, but big tears were trickling down her cheeks.

He dug in his pocket for a handkerchief and gave it to her. Then he stood, holding her head against his stomach. He half looked round at Jarvis, but spoke to Kate.

'I'm sorry, girl,' he said. 'I'm sorry.'

'What else?' asked Kate.

'Oh, I don't know,' said Jarvis. 'Let me see. One thing they will ask is which one of you was sick at the Pool of Time.'

'I was,' said Dunne, reddening.

'Oh, well,' said Jarvis. 'That was something else I had noticed. I'm not sure that the police had said anything about it. But it might have indicated that someone else had been there.'

'No smoke without a fire. No sick without a . . . a . . .' Dunne gave up his attempt to be light-hearted about it. 'Yes. I suppose it just might have been a clue.'

'Too fresh,' said Jarvis seriously, and then caught sight of Kate's expression. 'I'm sorry. Look, the bar will shut shortly. Can I get you two a drink.'

'It won't,' said Dunne placidly. 'The Commander came in while you were otherwise engaged, to announce that the bar would stay open as long as there was a demand, as he put it. Right under the police's noses too.' He laughed, and added, 'But I'll have a whisky, please.'

Jarvis looked at Kate as he prised himself up from the chair. She shook her head, indicating a half-full glass in front of her.

'This will do me,' she said.

At the bar Jarvis got Dunne's whisky, and dithered a bit himself before settling simply for three dry ginger ales in a large tumbler with ice. He was thirsty and also felt that anything stronger might just have a go at his gut. There was enough trouble down there already. Besides, he did not want to be put off his sleep. He also mentioned the dying fire.

He was just about to open the door into the lounge, when Earlston came out, bumping into him, and almost upsetting the ginger ale.

'Look where you're going,' Jarvis thought Earlston said as he went past, but it was said slurredly, and Earlston did not stop nor look back at Jarvis. He went up the stair, leaning against the wall as he went. Jarvis watched him go up the first flight. Then, remembering what Kate and Dunne had said about Earlston's unpredictability when affected by drink, he turned and went into the room.

He gave Dunne his whisky and settled down gingerly once more into the low chair.

'Earlston nearly ran me down,' he said in a mock-aggrieved tone. 'What is wrong with him?'

'Quite a lot,' said Dunne. 'Where do you want me to start? Basically, he's been left behind, and he blames other folk for it. The way I hear it, when he was the age to make a real mark, he spent the time dreaming of himself as a famous economist, another Balogh advising the government.'

'Not another Keynes?' asked Jarvis, with a lifted eyebrow.

'Not according to the other night,' replied Dunne wryly.

'He was hard done by,' Kate said quietly.

'He wasn't,' said Dunne. 'He's done nothing worth tuppence.'

'He's been left behind?' queried Jarvis.

'Precisely,' said Dunne. 'But he is convinced that it is all the fault of other people.'

'Is it?'

'No. He's had more consideration out of his seniors than anyone else I know. They've played him very lightly, and given stick to others.'

'Oh, come,' said Kate. 'That's too harsh. He's good at his job.'

'If Leith had been good at his job as head of department. Jack would have been in other employment years ago,' Dunne retorted. He stared at Kate.

She dropped her eyes, and, her hands twisting together in her lap, said, 'Yes. I suppose so.'

Dunne leaned back with some satisfaction.

There was a pause, then Jarvis probed again.

'And the row with Huntley?'

'All of a piece,' said Dunne expansively. 'In fact, they are somewhat alike. Huntley's done nothing either, really, but he has a way with the girls. Jack hasn't, and Huntley knows it, and Jack knows that Huntley knows it, and Huntley won't let go.'

'That's over now,' said Kate in a low voice.

Dunne paused, surprised by the interruption. 'I was forgetting.' Then with growing excitement he said, 'Maybe that's it. Maybe Jack pushed Ron into the river!'

'Ron?'

'Huntley.'

'I never knew his full name,' said Jarvis.

'You can't be serious,' said Kate.

'It would fit,' Dunne said. 'He's been odd this whole week. That episode outside your room was only a bit of it.'

'But there's Benedict as well,' replied the girl.

'Ah,' said Dunne, hunching forward as if playing a game of chess. 'Well, suppose old Benedict reported adversely on an article Jack had written, and that Jack got to know of it.'

'Did he?' asked Kate, interested despite herself.

'Yes,' said Dunne triumphantly. 'He torpedoed the article that Jack submitted recently to the *Aspen Journal*.'

'That wouldn't be a motive,' Jarvis objected.

'It could have been the last straw,' argued Dunne. 'I happen to know that Jack's thesis had to go to a third external examiner because Benedict, who was one of the first examiners, failed it. And Jack knew that.'

'But what about the other external? You told me the decision was unanimous,' said Jarvis.

'That's right. So I did.' Dunne leaned forward and dropped his voice. 'The other external was, I believe, Merrick of Worcester.'

'The one who's had a stroke?' inquired Jarvis.

'Yes,' said Dunne. 'As I understand it, he might have

permitted a re-write, so the PhD committee asked for a third opinion—from whom I do not know.'

Kate snorted. 'So your spies are not infallible.'

Dunne put out his tongue at her, and resumed. 'The third was also for failing the thing outright. So Jack thinks that Benedict was the crucial opinion in all that. And faced with the three recommendations, of course the committee went with the majority, especially since Benedict's view had been backed up.' He paused, then added, 'I wish I knew who the third was.'

There was a pause.

'Go on,' said Jarvis.

'Shortly after the thesis was failed there was an opening for a senior lecturer. It was known beforehand that it was coming up, and for some reason Jack had thought he would get it. He hadn't a hope really. Even with a PhD. But he's convinced that Benedict torpedoed him then as well. Apparently they didn't even take up his references. Leith told me that.'

'In confidence, no doubt,' said Kate bitterly. She got to her feet. 'I've had enough of this.'

'Please don't go. At any rate, please don't go in anger,' said Jarvis, without getting to his feet. 'I'm sure he's just letting his speculations have free rein, but means no harm.'

'He enjoys running folk down like that,' she replied less heatedly. 'I'm sure there's no truth in it at all.'

'We don't even know why the police are investigating,' said Jarvis disarmingly. 'Dunne here is talking in terms of murder, but that hasn't been said officially.'

'You looked too serious when you came in,' said Dunne defensively. 'Despite what you said.'

'Come on. Sit down,' said Jarvis. 'If you go off like that and leave me with him like this, I'll not get to sleep tonight for worrying.'

Kate laughed, and sank down again to her seat. 'All right. On condition that we talk of something else.'

'Very well. You choose,' said Jarvis.

She furrowed her brow, very prettily, Jarvis considered.

'What do you think should be done about South Africa?' she inquired after a little thought.

'How do you mean?' asked Jarvis.

'Sanctions or not?' said Kate. 'Or can we prosecute them before the International Court?'

Jarvis was rescued from having to correct her by the appearance of Mather. He brought a chair with him from beside the door, and sat with it reversed, leaning on his crossed arms on top of its back.

'Ladies and gentlemen,' said Dunne. 'Please put your hands together for tonight's star turn, Buffalo Pete Mather, who will astound you with his feats with a Winchester rifle, a Colt handgun, and a pea-shooter. Hoorah!'

Mather, Jarvis and Kate laughed, and Mather played it up a little, pretending first to quell a bucking steed, and then to shade his eyes against the desert sun.

'Howdy,' he said.

But Kate leaned over, took the remains of Dunne's whisky from him, and put it on the floor beside her seat on the other side from Dunne. 'You've had enough,' she said. Then she looked up. The constable was approaching their table.

'Dr Greenway?'

She got up and followed him.

'Good luck,' called Dunne, and blew a kiss.

13

When Kate had gone, Dunne looked at Mather. 'All right. Spill the beans.'

'Nothing to spill,' said Mather somewhat primly.

'Come off it,' said Dunne. 'What were they asking?'

'If I might say so,' interrupted Jarvis, 'that is precisely what I was saying. We really are better not to discuss it, at least until everyone has seen the police.'

'You discussed it yourself when you came back,' Dunne said hotly.

'Not really. Think back.'

After a pause Dunne agreed. 'I suppose you told us damn-all, really. And I suppose my theories weren't discussing it either.'

Jarvis spread his hand, palm up, and shrugged.

'Well, what shall we talk about?' asked Dunne. 'It really is very artificial to ignore why we are sitting here and not in our pits snoring it out.'

'Tell me . . . tell me what your Vice-Chancellor is like,' said Jarvis.

Mather snorted. 'You have a talent for picking on inexhaustible topics,' he said with a laugh. 'Go on, Jim. Let fly.'

Dunne did.

Not very long elapsed, however, before Kate Greenway returned and Dunne himself was summoned. He left, jauntily. The others remained waiting for him in a companionable silence, talk more or less exhausted. Other groups started to split up.

After a few had very obviously left for bed the Inspector came in and intimated that there would be no more interviews that night, since things were running late, but that the police would be back in the morning and would resume their interviewing after breakfast.

'Interesting,' said Jarvis. 'Very interesting.'

The others looked at him.

'Unless I am much mistaken,' he said, 'we four have been interviewed by the Superintendent himself and he has seen no one else. But he is shutting things down now.'

'That's right,' said Kate. 'It was you first and we followed in order. What does that mean?' She looked worried.

'Probably nothing at all,' said Jarvis. 'The common thread would seem to be that we were the ones involved

first with each body.' He paused. 'I wonder if they saw
Anderson before they came on here?'

'It doesn't mean that . . . that . . .'

'No, of course it doesn't mean they are specially interested
in us, it is just that they have clearly decided that one team
will interview those who are clearly, as it were, associated
with the events. Then they can sift the reports from the
other team once they think they have a basic understanding
to work from.'

'Well, they're taking too long,' said Mather. 'I'm getting
very tired.' He looked weary.

'Off you go, if you like,' said Jarvis.

'I'll stay and wait for Jim,' said Kate.

'We'll keep you company,' said Mather, visibly trying to
brighten himself up. 'I can stand another few minutes.'

'We're all tired,' Jarvis said, yawning. 'It has all been a
shock, particularly for you three finding Benedict. In each
case I arrived knowing that there was a body. Nor indeed,
did I know them very well.' He shook his head. 'And yet,
you know, I strangely regret Benedict.'

Dunne came back. The spring was gone from his step.
He fell into his chair, rather than sat down.

'Phew,' he said. 'They're a couple of terriers.'

'What happened?' asked Kate. 'They were pleasant
enough with me.'

'They grilled me,' said Dunne, with a recovering fierce-
ness. 'First it was almost step by step up to that Pot and
then what happened thereafter. Then I mentioned that I
thought that there were various people who did not like
Benedict.'

'Oh, Jim!' exclaimed Kate.

'I know. I know. Or at least I know now.' He turned
to Jarvis. 'You were right. I should have stuck to today's
facts.'

'I didn't say that.

'Someone did. If you didn't, you should have. No matter.

They were on to what I said.' He leaned back and looked apologetically at Kate.

'I'm sorry, girl,' he went on. 'I told them about Jack and about his relationship with Benedict and with Huntley. And about the other night. And about the scenes here with both of them. And the scene between Huntley and Benedict.' He buried his head in his hands.

'A mine of information,' Mather observed drily.

'Well,' said Jarvis, 'you never know. I could tell them nothing, but there were those undercurrents. It may help.'

'But won't that make them the more suspicious about what were clearly accidents?' asked Kate.

Jarvis sighed. 'Were they?'

Kate looked at him, and somehow seemed to shrink into her seat.

'Weren't they?' she asked in a small voice.

'I understand,' said Jarvis carefully, and lowering his voice so that only the immediate company heard what he said, 'I understand that there were injuries to Benedict which are unlikely to be compatible with accident, and that there is also some doubt about Huntley.'

'Wow-ee!' drawled Dunne, recovering his bounce. 'And this from the man who would tell us nothing.'

'Shush!' said Kate. 'That was before we had all seen the Inspector.

'Superintendent,' Jarvis corrected absently.

'You do know a lot more than you are telling us,' said Kate. The form was a statement, but the inflection made it into a question.

Jarvis strove to deflect the mistrust he saw growing in her eyes.

'There is a professional relationship, I suppose,' he replied. 'In a way we are both working with the law. They did let me know that there were grounds for concern, but I would ask that you don't let it go further. I shouldn't have said as much as I have, and it is sufficient to justify the police being here that there have been two deaths in a short period almost in the same place.'

'Well, I've had enough,' said Dunne. 'No. I am not angry. It's just that I'm pooped.' He got to his feet.

'Me too,' said Kate, and also rose.

Jarvis had had his back to the room, and was surprised when he got up to find that there was no one else left. Mather caught his surprise.

'They all started to leave when they were told that that was it for the night.'

'Oh, well,' said Jarvis. 'I'll take the glasses back to the bar.'

There was a tray lying on one of the tables, and he and Mather went round collecting the few glasses that were left in the room. Dunne and Greenway went off. Mather followed, going up the main stairs, while Jarvis carried the tray along the corridor to the bar. The bar had shut, so he left the tray on the shelf of the hatch. Then he went up the back stairs to go to his room.

As he turned left at the upper landing to go along the corridor to his room, he heard the sound of crying coming from one of the rooms on his right. He went along to investigate.

He stopped and listened, his ear close to the door of the room that it was coming from. He could not make out anything other than that there was someone in great distress in that room.

He knocked.

The sobbing stopped. 'Go away,' said a voice. It was Earlston.

Jarvis stood, silent, and heard sounds indicating that someone had crossed the room to stand equally silent behind the door.

'Are you all right?' asked Jarvis at last.

'Go away,' the voice repeated.

Jarvis did so.

When he reached his room, he found Superintendent Mason was sitting on his bed.

14

'I'm not here,' said Mason.

'I don't see you,' said Jarvis, coming into the room and taking off his jacket and shoes. 'I'm going to bed.'

'I am wondering why you are here,' said Mason.

'I am wondering why *you* are here,' replied Jarvis.

'I am here because I am wondering why you are here,' said the other.

'I am here to go to bed,' said Jarvis flatly.

'Immediately, yes,' said the Superintendent. 'But in the broader context of the week?'

'You have checked my booking?'

'Of course.'

'I told you,' replied Jarvis.

'On oath you would have to tell the truth, the whole truth, and nothing but the truth.'

'The only oath you are likely to hear from me is otherwise worded.'

'But then I'm not here.'

Jarvis started to undress.

Mason sat him out, silently, and Jarvis sat down, shirtless and trouserless, on the seat beside the bedroom table.

'If I were here for reasons additional to the ones I have given you, I would not be at liberty to indicate them,' Jarvis said at last.

Mason grunted, got to his feet and went across to the window. The moon was high.

'Official Secrets Act?' he said.

'Now there is a possibility, though the probability is greater that I am here for a holiday, a break from pushing back the horizons of knowledge.'

'Section one, or section two,' mused Mason.

Jarvis did not reply.

'I am intrigued,' said Mason. 'Usually in a situation like this I would think, or my boss would think, of getting in touch with London, just in case there was something. After all, a case, or cases, involving a raft of academics of varied origin just might raise matters other than that of the run of the mill.'

'I like that description,' said Jarvis. 'A raft of academics. The raft seems to be getting smaller—I mean in the general provision, not in the area of your current investigations. Though I suppose it might come to that. Some of the things said with the cuts in financing have been pretty severe. It might come to throwing folk overboard.'

Mason ignored the pleasantry, and went on, 'but in this case, London has got in touch with us, and that is not usual of itself.' He turned. 'Would you, perchance, have made any phone calls since these events unfolded?'

'Not admitted.'

The Superintendent barked a laugh. 'I did a law degree. The form is "not known and not admitted".'

'Not admitted,' Jarvis repeated.

'In that case we may be on the same side, though I was beginning to have doubts.'

'I am on the side of the angels, and even law and order.'

'In that case, perhaps you could tell me whatever you may have heard, or deduced, about the relationships of either of the dead men with anyone else here.'

'I thought you always said "deceased", not "dead". But I was glad Dunne told you what he did.'

'He talked, did he? He is a bit of a blether, but there was similar information from the others. Come on. Give. I am not here, you recall. But there is no reason why you shouldn't talk to yourself or to the walls. It is expected of academics. I'll just be a fly on the wall.'

'You mean a blue-bottle,' said Jarvis wryly. 'All right.

On the basis that you are not here, and that I have no notion that I am being overheard.'

'Maybe you could check that first,' said Mason, indicating the door.

'Are you serious?' Jarvis saw from Mason's pointing finger that he was. He got up and went across the room, opened the door, and looked both ways along the corridor. It was empty.

He came back in and shrugged his shoulders. 'No one.'

'Perhaps you could start, then.'

Jarvis ran quickly over what he had gathered of the various relationships, concluding, 'But all that is hearsay, of course.'

'I know what hearsay is,' said Mason a little sharply, then added in a more conciliatory tone, 'That's not bad. If you want a job, let me know.'

'Fair's fair,' replied Jarvis. 'Tell me: did you visit Anderson before you came here?'

The Superintendent smiled. 'You'll do,' he said. 'Yes. We went to him first, but you'll be pleased to know that his story and yours agree in so far as they overlap.'

'Thanks.'

'Do you know why you are here?' said Mason genially.

'I am here on holiday. I was told there was interesting company, but I know no more than that.'

'Not as a bodyguard or supervisor?'

'Do I look like a bodyguard?'

'No. I suppose not. What about supervision?'

'Not even that. There was "interesting company", no more than that.'

'Was.' Mason had picked up the slightly stressed verb.

Jarvis said nothing.

'Well, it would seem unlikely that Huntley was company such that London might be interested. So that leaves our expatriate deceased.'

'No comment.'

'But not denied.'

Mason waited, saw that there would be no reply, and went on. 'That muddies the water somewhat—if you will excuse that language. So there might be extraneous involvement. On the other hand it could be a simple murder, for professional jealousy or the like. Or there might be a maniac among you.'

'Or among the local population.'

'True. But we have had nothing like this. So we will proceed for the present on the assumption that the killer came into the area with the conference. Or on holiday, like yourself.'

'If you are being that logical, it is also possible that you have two killers, or that one case at least was an accident. Huntley could have struck his head on his way into the water.'

'Remotely possible,' said Mason. 'Our ghoul tells me that, if he had struck his head on his way in, Huntley's autonomic nervous system would probably have still caused him to breathe at least once after the blow.'

'Oh.'

'That is why what you have told me of the conference party is useful. Some of it I had gathered already, and some confirms other information. But there is a good bit more. There was something between Benedict and Dr Pont, I understand. But she is too shattered to be the killer—the last time she saw him they argued about the proofs of a joint article which came up by train urgently, the other day.'

'Ah.'

'A number of other folk here this week had no cause to like either Benedict or Huntley. Benedict because he had been—well, the polite way to put it would be that he didn't suffer fools, gladly or otherwise. Huntley seems to have been in a permanent state of rut and argument. I don't know. You academic folk are supposed to be the intelligent ones, and you are like a lot of spoiled brats.'

'Guilty,' said Jarvis. 'At least for a lot of us. There is a prima donna in each of us just busting to get out.'

'My impression when I was going through my university course was that you folk really are pretty ordinary, but with pretensions. That said, there are some of you that justify the airs. But a lot don't.'

'I know, I know.' Jarvis stood up and stretched. 'Now,' he said, 'I'm sorry, but I really am bushed.'

'Who was that crying down the lane?' Mason asked suddenly.

'Little Johnny Earlston.'

'Was it now,' said Mason slowly.

'Yes.'

'Figure of speech.'

'I know. But really, I am dead beat.'

'All right. I'll probably see you tomorrow.'

Mason left the room, and Jarvis hurried to bed. But sleep was a long time in coming. It took two antacids to make his gut comfortable.

SIX: SATURDAY

1

His alarm, which he forgotten to turn off, startled him. Jarvis awoke with a bad taste in his mouth, and the beginnings of a headache. He felt awful, his pyjamas clammy, and aches in his arms and legs.

He got up and cleaned his teeth, scrubbing them while looking into the mirror over the basin, but conscious as he did so of the dark bags under his eyes and the shiny texture to his skin. He washed. That helped a good bit, but even so on closer inspection his eyes looked unhealthy, their usual whiteness clouded. Some holiday, he thought.

It had been wet overnight, and a morning mist lay on the field, but to no great depth. From his vantage-point it looked as though the cows were wading in a white pool, and from that curious scene he deduced that it might still be chilly outside. He could see no one.

He dressed, putting on a scarf as well as his raincoat, preparing for his morning walk. It struck him that he was getting to be as regular in his habits as Benedict. He grinned mirthlessly to himself, remembering the admonition to possible assassination targets never to be predictable, always to vary routes and times. He wondered briefly if that sort of thought had ever occurred to Benedict. But then, he told himself, Benedict had not known he was a target. Or had he? What was the reason for his exhilaration the night before his death? Had it been premonition, as Milton had felt? He himself had had some thoughts on those lines. He wondered if he had mentioned that to Mason the night before.

The thought of Mason triggered other thoughts. Had he

been indiscreet in what he had said? No. At least not in the culpable sense, for by that curious message transmitted through the Superintendent, George Appleby had told him to reveal whatever his own judgement indicated as desirable.

Oh well, it's done now, he told himself, and left his room.

The vestibule was deserted, and the papers had not yet arrived on the shelf of polished Victorian wood.

It was chilly, and he was glad of coat and scarf. A misty sun was rising, but as yet gave no heat.

Going down the slight slope of the drive to where the path branched off for the river, he found himself reluctant to take that familiar route. Instead he strode on, down the avenue of beeches, with the intention of going into the village. Perhaps, he thought, he would be able to get a local newspaper and see what the outside world was making of the happenings at Ebony House.

As he came in sight of the lodge at the gate to the avenue he saw the first puffs rise from its chimney. Someone was up and doing, lighting the fire for the new day.

At the gate itself he was met by a raincoated and cold-looking police constable.

'Good morning, sir,' said the constable. 'Not a very good morning, I'm afraid, but not bad for the time of year.'

Jarvis stopped.

'Would you be from the house?' asked the constable.

'Yes.'

'I wonder, sir, if you would mind just telling me your name, and giving me an indication of where you are going?'

'Jarvis. I'm out on my usual morning walk, and thought I might get a paper in the village.'

'I see, sir. Could you give me a moment?' The constable moved back a little distance and spoke, head bent, into a microphone tucked inside his coat. Jarvis could not make out what he said, but heard the crackle of a reply.

'That's fine, sir,' said the policeman, coming back. 'You know the way?'

'Would you have stopped me?' asked Jarvis.

'Oh no, sir, That would not be lawful.' The constable smiled.

'But perhaps someone would appear further down the road just to check who I was?'

The constable smiled, but said nothing.

'How would you suspect a false name?'

The constable continued to smile.

'OK,' said Jarvis. 'I'll be back shortly.' He stuffed his hands in his pockets against the chill.

'Inspector Paget sends his compliments,' said the constable, with a broader smile.

Jarvis snorted a laugh himself, and set off. Down at the first corner in the road after the bridge, he spotted a car tucked in down a farm lane, and waved cheerfully to the two men sitting inside it. One waved back.

In the village the paper shop had just opened, and two paper boys were setting off on their rounds as Jarvis arrived. He bought a copy of the *Birley Courier*, and the *Greyhavens Gazette*, and took them to a seat in the square.

It did not take long to discover that the drowning of Huntley had a brief mention in both papers, but the news about Benedict must have broken too late for either, that was if the news had broken at all. In news-gathering terms Ebony House would be an isolated spot. Still, no doubt that would change.

He got up and went round to the phone-box. The duty officer duly took a note of what he reported about his official interview with Mason. However, he could give Jarvis no information whatsoever. It was difficult to tell over the phone, of course, but Jarvis did feel that the man genuinely knew nothing about the matter, and was not dissembling.

Jarvis asked that Appleby be available to talk the next day.

'I'll call after I've been to church,' he said. 'Ask him either to be in the office, or you folk be ready to patch my call through.'

'After what?' asked the voice, surprised. 'This seems to be a bad line.'

'After church,' repeated Jarvis.

'That's what I thought you said,' said the officer.

Jarvis walked back, whistling. The car was still there, and the constable gave him a smile and a brisk salute as he passed him.

'Am I the only chicken out of the coop?' Jarvis asked.

''Fraid so, sir. There's no one gone out anywhere except yourself.'

Jarvis stopped, frowning.

'I'm sure you aren't supposed to tell me things like that,' he said.

'Like what,' said the constable blandly.

Inspector Paget appeared from the lodge.

Jarvis looked at him, and then at the constable, who seemed entirely unworried about whether Jarvis might ask an embarrassing question or not.

Paget forestalled him.

'We have been told by the Superintendent,' he said, 'that yourself is to be treated as having an unofficial status.'

'Oh,' said Jarvis. 'I see. Or at least I don't, but I suppose that doesn't matter.'

Paget looked at his watch. 'You've been the only one out this morning,' he said. 'And if you want to get your porridge and toast warm, you had better hurry.'

'Maybe Annie would find something for me,' replied Jarvis with a smile.

'You could tell her, if you see her, that we'll be up about

nine-thirty and working through the morning. There will
be an extra couple of us as well.'

'Tea or coffee?' Jarvis asked wryly.

'She knows what we need, but I don't know about the
new ones. They're down from Greyhavens.'

'I'll tell her,' said Jarvis, intrigued that outsiders had
apparently been called in.

'By the way,' he added as he was leaving, 'are there any
restrictions, formal or informal on those of us you have seen
already? It would be a useful break for us to go somewhere
this afternoon, say up the valley to the castle and the
loch.'

'I'll ask,' said the Inspector, going back into the lodge.

2

Jarvis was indeed late for breakfast, as Paget had proph-
esied. Mather, Dunne and Greenway were leaving the
dining-room just as he was entering, and it was clear from
the empty places and general chaos in the room that most
of the conference had already breakfasted.

He settled at his table with his cornflakes, and was adding
the milk when Milton came in. A night's sleep had done
wonders for him.

'What's been going on?' asked Milton, carrying his plate
over to Jarvis's table.

'What do you know?'

'Not a thing. I went upstairs and took a pill. This is the
first of me. But I saw Mather outside just now. He said you
would bring me up to date.'

Jarvis silently called down a minor affliction on Mather,
and then wondered what he might say. Milton had had
enough shocks already, despite his apparent freshness this
morning. He decided that brevity would be best.

'There was a team of policemen here all evening after
dinner,' he said.

To his surprise Milton accepted the statement without question.

'Yes,' he replied. 'I suppose that there would have to be. Two in one day would call for some inquiries, wouldn't it?' He looked up puckishly from his rice krispies. 'And did they indicate what they were looking for?'

'Not in detail.'

'Oh dear,' said Milton. 'You know, before I fell asleep I worked out a theory.' He looked down at his plate again. 'It is dreadful to say so, but you know that yesterday I thought Benedict might have committed suicide?'

'Yes.'

'Well, I have come to the conclusion that he would not have done that . . . at least not just yet.'

Jarvis looked puzzled.

'You see,' went on Milton, putting down his spoon, and leaning on his elbows, 'Benedict has been . . .' He hesitated and resumed, 'had been invited to deliver the London Academy Lecture next month. It is very prestigious, and I cannot see that he would have given that up.'

'He was very excited,' said Jarvis.

'I know, I know. But he did get excited. However, I still cannot see yesterday's events and that invitation going together. He was too proud for that.'

'Even if something disastrous had come up?'

'If you mean he might have behaved in a dramatic Eastern European manner, I suppose that is true. But if that were the case he would have left a letter stating the whole matter.'

'I haven't heard of one, but the police did seal his room. In any event I suppose a letter could be in the post to someone.'

'Let's hope it is first class.' Milton surprised Jarvis with a chuckle as he spoke.

'I think . . .' said Jarvis, and hesitated. 'Perhaps you should tell the police what you think—that is, what you have just said to me, when you talk to Superintendent Mason later on this morning.'

'I?'

'They are interviewing everybody. They are trying to deal first with those who must leave early, and the Commander has agreed that those who can, can stay on over the weekend. It will make things that bit easier all round.'

'Oh dear,' said Milton. 'I hadn't thought of that. I am expected at home by six. There is a meeting this evening that I am speaking at.'

'I'm sure that will be quite all right. There will be someone in the main hall to arrange that, if they do things the same way as they did yesterday. I'm sure they won't need to keep you for very long. Though I would also say that I think they will want to ask you something about the professional relationships between the people here.'

Milton's mouth twisted downwards. 'Yes. I can see that that would be of interest. I could be here until Monday just talking about all that, and even then that is only one man's view.'

'I'm sure it won't take that long. Just tell them what you think is relevant, and then cope with any questions they put to expand things.'

'I hope it won't take too long. But I suppose that when there are two deaths it takes time to deal with it. At least up here you civilized people don't have the Coroner.'

'No,' said Jarvis, surprised.

'Damned historical survival,' said Milton. 'Would be better in a zoo, or in a bottle.'

Jarvis looked surprised.

'My brother-in-law is one,' Milton added. 'He's a pompous buffoon.'

Out in the vestibule, Jarvis and Milton found that the police had arrived, and had already begun their sequence of interviews. However, when they approached the constable at the table, he at once said that Superintendent Mason was waiting to see Professor Milton, if that was convenient.

Milton agreed, and was shown into the office. Clearly there were other interviews going on in the library, and on his return the constable said that they were also using a small room down the corridor beyond the bar.

'Many to go?' asked Jarvis.

'No,' said the constable.

Jarvis was looking at the Ordnance Survey map on the wall, deciding where to propose the walk in the afternoon when Mather, Dunne and Greenway came out from the lounge. They came over to him and watched as he silently traced with his finger the path from the car park at the head of the valley, round past the castle, along to the ruined church beside the loch, and then along the side of the loch.

'I was going to suggest that we have a walk up there this afternoon, if you folk are not leaving. I have asked the constabulary,' said Jarvis.

'We're not leaving,' said Mather. 'Not today. It seems that each of us was specifically asked if we could stay on, in case there were other things to cross-check.'

'Well, then?'

'Good idea,' said Dunne. 'I'm beginning to feel cooped up.'

Greenway had other things on her mind. Throughout the discussion she had been biting her lip.

'Was Jack Earlston in for breakfast when you were in?' she asked Jarvis.

'Look,' said Dunne angrily, 'I've told you he's not a child, though he behaves like one. Let him alone. You cannot play nursemaid.'

Kate continued to look at Jarvis, heedless of Dunne.

'No, he wasn't,' said Jarvis slowly, wondering where this would lead.

'There you are,' said Kate to Dunne. 'I'm going up to see.'

'Don't be a fool,' he called after her, and then turned, sheepish, as the constable looked up. 'About that walk,' he said. 'We need only take my car. It's the biggest.'

'How about footwear?' Mather asked. 'It is probably still quite muddy up there.'

'I'm all right,' said Jarvis.

'So am I,' said Dunne, lifting his feet to show thick rubber soles on stout shoes.

'What about Kate?' asked Mather.

'I don't know,' said Dunne.

'What size does she take? I've got a pair of Wellington boots in the car, and my feet are pretty small.'

'But beautifully in proportion,' grinned Dunne, patting the smaller man on the head.

Mather took a good-natured swing at him, but it never landed, for a scream came from the upper corridor.

The three, followed by the constable, raced upstairs and along the corridor, and found Kate standing at the open door of Earlston's room. Dunne grabbed her and turned her face against him. He looked over the top of her head.

'My God!' he said, and twisting, pulled her back into the corridor.

Jarvis pushed past and went into the room, followed by the constable. He heard Mather outside say, 'What's the matter?'

Earlston was lying with his head in a pool of blood on the parquet flooring beside the window at the opposite side of the narrow room. He seemed to have struggled a bit, for he still had the fringe of the bedspread in his hand and it was partly pulled from the bed which lay along one wall.

'Stay here,' said the constable. 'Don't let anyone in.' He went out, partly closing the door.

'Thanks very much,' said Jarvis wearily to the door. Then he approached the twisted body, careful to touch nothing.

There was a knife on the floor, a bone-handled knife with a curved, vicious-looking blade. It was slightly stained. The pool of blood proved to be exactly that, though, seen closer, it was darkened to brown and to some extent had seeped into the flooring.

Jarvis leaned over the body, feeling sick. It was face up. He looked for the tell-tale sign, and it was there in the shape of several small cuts above and below the gash which clearly had been the cause of death.

'You will find,' his mind replayed the high-pitched voice of Hughes, who had lectured to him on Forensic Medicine. 'You will find that often in the ordinary case of suicide by these means, there are a few tentative cuts and then the final one, made with some strength. One might almost say, conviction, gentlemen.'

Jarvis looked round. Now that he was into the room he saw that there were some bloodstains on the wash-hand basin.

He pictured to himself the unhappy Earlston standing at the mirror, as he himself had stood earlier that morning when doing his teeth. But Earlston had not had a brush in hand, but a knife. Then he envisaged him pivoting and falling, his hand catching the end of the bed.

He wondered at what point of decision Earlston had been when he had heard him the night before. Had he had the knife in his hand? Or did the decision come later, when the unhappy man had heard the footsteps recede along the corridor, leaving him alone. Alone. What might have happened if Jarvis had tried the door? If it had been open? It probably had been, for he could not imagine Earlston unlocking it and then going to the mirror with the knife.

Jarvis shuddered, and came back to stand beside the door.

3

The waters of the loch were blue, a blue that would be incredible in a watercolour, and yet here seemed entirely right. The blue was offset by the dull green and yellow of the tussocky moorland grass which covered the steep slopes opposite. On the nearer side the darker greens and browns of the heather interspersed with blisters of weathered reddish granite rolled gently down to that startling blue. Only the gash of the bulldozed Land-Rover track along the north side was intrusive. Still, if you hunkered down against the huge erratic which some glacier had left perched high at the bend in the valley, you could avoid seeing that reddish wound running up the side of the loch.

Mather and Jarvis did so, looking down the length of the loch and across at the slopes. The boulder sheltered them from the slight but chilling wind, which turned the corner from the remaining and higher loch-less third of the valley. Beside them a rutted track led down to the end of the loch over a flimsy-seeming bridge and on across the valley floor to a white-painted farmhouse which, sheltered by trees, stood on a small plateau formed by a stream which still sparkled its way down beside the little field it had created.

They had come there in silence. By unspoken consent nothing had been said during the drive up the valley from Ebony House, nor had they spoken during the long three and a bit miles to where they now sheltered.

At length Mather straightened, burrowed inside his driving jacket and fetched out a small pair of binoculars. He began to scan the slopes opposite. Soon he grunted, and, without lowering the binoculars, gestured with one hand in the general direction he was looking in. Jarvis dug out his own binoculars from inside his windcheater. He checked the relative focusing against the trees beside the white farmhouse and then followed Mather's indication.

There were deer over there, picking their careful way

across the slope. As he watched, one jumped across what was clearly a swampy patch round a small spring. The deer were nervous, seemingly conscious of the human presence even though so far away. Each bent to graze but raised its head watchfully almost with each bite. When chewing, each head was turned to gaze across and down at the intruders.

Jarvis continued to scan across the face of the slope, along its crest, and along above the white farm and across the bluff up which ran the zigzag of the path to the high moor. His view came to the outcrop of reddish rock stained with brown, green and yellow streaks from the water seeping down from the peat moss which, he knew, lay in the bowl above, hidden from their view. Then he panned upwards into that startling sky.

He nudged Mather and pointed. Mather followed and whistled softly. A buzzard was circling above the rock-face, black against the brightness.

'Watch your eyes with the sun,' said Jarvis quietly.

Mather nodded.

After a time, as if rehearsed, the two resumed their semi-squat against the rock, looking out and down the length of the loch.

A little while later, by another unspoken signal they got to their feet and started back.

When they got to the little ruined church nestling in its churchyard down by the shore of the loch, Mather half raised his arm, indicating that he wanted to have a look at it. Jarvis followed him across the sheep-cropped turf, avoiding the splotches of sheep dirt that were scattered about.

The old, green-painted iron gate squealed as it opened and the two entered the graveyard. Jarvis walked across to the wall beside the loch and stood looking back up the loch, while Mather wandered about looking at various of the ancient gravestones. Jarvis got out his binoculars again, and swept the valley, bracing his elbows on the low wall which was at a convenient height to act as a prop.

At length Mather came and joined him.

'I didn't realize the water came that close,' he said, looking over at the wavelets lapping the base of the wall.

Jarvis lowered his binoculars.

'You know,' he said, 'I've been here often, and I knew it well when I was a student. I used to get a holiday job on the next estate. It marches with this one. We were grouse-beating mostly, and used to come along that edge there.' He indicated the high ridge to his left, along whose slopes the deer had moved. 'It hasn't changed. Nothing has really changed. The trees have grown a bit, and that boathouse has been repaired.' He pointed to a low building which Mather had not noticed, couching low against the bank of the loch to his left. 'Man comes and goes, but the land never changes.'

He pointed back up the loch to where the white farm could still be seen, no more than a dot at the distance. 'Away up that ladder, and out on to the high moor, there's the remains of a plane. It was either practising low-flying, or was careless or something. But it's still up there. It was the further end of one of the traverses on the furthest beat. I remember Ian John the game-keeper used to look round the group when he was telling us how we had to line off on each beat. When it was up there he would look round, and then point at someone.' Jarvis pointed, his thumb erect, so that his hand mimicked a pistol.

'You,' he said in a high scratchy tone. 'You'll go round the RAF.' He rolled the 'R'. 'And you would have to do it. You had to go like the devil to get round that part quick enough not to slow the line, and it was mostly across bog. You were lucky if you came off without at least a bootful of ooze, and sometimes more.' He grinned at the memory, and then his face darkened. 'I suppose Ian John is gone now, and even one of those I used to come with has gone as well.'

He turned slowly on his heel, taking in the ancient scene. 'And yet,' he said, 'for all our fun and effort, there is not a trace, and even the plane wreck had just about rotted all those years ago. I expect it's vanished now. But these hills and the loch don't change.'

'Man makes change,' said Mather pointing to the slash of the track down which they had trudged.

'A few more years and that will not be visible.'

'Unless it causes erosion.'

Jarvis grimaced.

'Yet look at all these graves,' said Mather, turning to the churchyard. 'There must have been quite a community here a couple of hundred years ago, enough to have their own church.'

'And school,' said Jarvis. 'Did you see the schoolmaster's grave?'

Mather shook his head, and Jarvis took him over to the plot.

'And now they have all gone,' Mather mused.

Jarvis looked round at the graveyard, the stones level with the grass, and the few still erect.

'I heard him crying last night,' he said at last.

Mather said nothing.

'I was outside his door. When you and the others went upstairs I went up the back stairs from the bar. I heard him crying in his room. I knocked and he told me to go away.'

Mather reached out and gripped him by the shoulder.

Jarvis looked directly at him.

'I went away,' he said, slowly and distinctly.

'Pray it out,' said Mather suddenly, in a clipped tone, and he dropped his hand and turned away embarrassed, his face flushing red.

Jarvis gave vent to a shout of laughter, and Mather flinched.

'Don't,' said Jarvis. 'Don't. I'm not laughing at you. I am laughing at myself. Here am I trying . . . trying to purge . . . to purge my conscience among the changeless hills, and I could have got the cure anywhere.'

Mather turned to him, relieved, though his face was still flushed.

'Sometimes I speak before I think.'

'It was rightly said.'

But, notwithstanding his words, a constraint came down upon them. Mather looked at his watch, and Jarvis checked his. They set off back to the car.

When they were getting into it, Jarvis said abruptly, 'I hope Kate Greenway is all right.'

Mather grinned, in relief that the tension had broken.

'It's been good to see Jim taking care of her. I hope it makes him see sense. He needs someone like her.'

Jarvis nodded, but could not suppress a sigh.

Mather looked quizzically at him, but Jarvis pretended to be busy fixing his seat-belt.

4

It was a subdued evening. When Jarvis and Mather returned to Ebony House it was to find that Superintendent Mason and his team had completed their interviews, and that some of the conference had already left. Professor Milton had apparently been taken by police car to the train at Birley and should have made the necessary connection on his way south, although he had not gone on the early train. It seemed that Earlston's death had resulted in some extra questions for him, and also for Greenway and Dunne. Mason was to return after dinner to see Jarvis and Mather.

The four once again sat together at dinner. Kate Greenway seemed a good bit better than when Jarvis had last seen her outside Earlston's door that morning. Dunne, by contrast, seemed to have had some of the bounce knocked out of him, and it was a much more serious person who sat down to dinner. In fact, irreverently, Jarvis found himself thinking that this perhaps would have been how Tigger would have been if Rabbit had succeeded in his plan to 'un-bounce' him. But then he thought that was unfair. Then he wondered whether it was unfair to Tigger or to Dunne, and spluttered into his soup.

Dunne carefully banged him on the back.

'Sorry. Gone down the wrong way,' Jarvis managed at last, but offered no other explanation.

Mather, however, rose to the occasion, droning on about the wonders of the scenery, the deer and the buzzard, the traces of the remains of civilization and what Sir Walter Scott might have done with such a setting. Sheltered by that wave of words, Jarvis was able to recover his composure.

It was clear that no one wanted to talk about recent events. There was an air, not so much of depression as of sheer listlessness in the room. Everyone knew that one of their number had done himself to death in a room not far from where each had been asleep, or staring at the ceiling, or reading a book, that previous night.

The room was virtually silent. It was not a companionable silence in the good and mellow sense in which such words are usually taken. It was companionable, but the companionship lay in shared misery. Shared, yet each was locked away in his or her own feelings about its cause.

It was therefore a relief when the meal finished. Looking at his watch, Jarvis realized, with that odd part of his mind which always seemed to be a detached observer, that the dinner had been the fastest in the week. No one had lingered over any mouthful, excellent though the fare had been.

They went through to the lounge, but were only settling when the young constable—Ian, Jarvis remembered—came to inform Mather that Superintendent Mason would be grateful if he could have a word with him.

Mather was not gone long, and then it was Jarvis's turn.

Mason took him briefly through the events of the morning, nodding at intervals as Jarvis ticked off the events as he remembered them. His colleague, seated in the armchair beside the fire as before, made notes.

'And do you have anything else for me?' inquired Mason with a slight smile, as the interview clearly drew to a close.

'Nothing.'

'You had a good walk this morning?'

Jarvis smiled. 'Had you people on all the exits?'

'Of course.'

'Why? Were you hoping that someone's nerve might break?'

'Maybe it did. Maybe it did,' breathed Mason. Then he said briskly, 'I would hope that if you were perhaps to receive any information which could be of assistance, you would also get permission to pass it on. We are dealing with a murder inquiry.'

'A murder?' Jarvis stressed the first word.

'A murder,' said Mason. 'A few murders. We don't yet know. But it does seem plain that this morning, this early morning, was a suicide.' He looked keenly at Jarvis.

'Yes,' replied Jarvis. 'That seems clear enough.' Then he asked. 'Any notes in any of the rooms?'

'Not a thing. Benedict's was a bit peculiar. It was so tidy. His case was packed, and the bedding carefully stacked. Just as if he were leaving.'

'I had not heard him say anything about going.'

'Nor had Pont, or Milton. In fact, Milton understood that he might stay on for a day or so if that were possible, but he had said nothing about that to the Commander.'

'Odd.'

'People are,' said Mason, with a smile. 'Well, if you hear anything . . .'

'So you are no closer?'

'Not really. We have had a second opinion on Huntley, and there is some evidence that he might have been struck a blow on the back of the head by a sharpish instrument, or a stone. But we don't really know. It is an inference from a site examination as well as looking at the skull. There is an injury consistent with a sharp or sharpish point, and the walls of the gorge are all smooth, so far as they can be seen. But we just cannot tell. We have, however, had a couple of our men check the edge of the gorge itself. And I mean the edge. We had them go over it on hands and knees, roped and guyed, of course, but they found nothing.'

'Hunch?'

'The closest I can come is that the suicide did both and then himself. He was clearly quite unstable, and there is evidence of rows, malevolence and opportunity. I am told that he had been conducting attacks on Benedict by letters to various journals, none of which would print what he had written, it was so clearly wrong. We are getting copies of some at least of these shortly. As for the other, it seems he enjoyed tormenting Earlston, casting doubt on his—what is it they call it nowadays?—his orientation. To say nothing of his professional capacity.'

Jarvis nodded. 'Not open and shut,' he said.

'No. But it began to look like the best we can do. So we have let most of the folk go. They clearly had no interest in the matter. And I really think we have no cause to detain anyone else who may have other things to go to.'

He paused, and looked round the room, as if saying goodbye to it, then turned to Jarvis.

'The one thing that keeps coming back to me is that you were here and I do not know exactly why. If London had said nothing, I would not be interested, but they contacted us. Why? Why? There is something nagging there.'

'Perhaps there is an explanation,' said Jarvis slowly. 'I used to be in work other than my present employment, and withdrew from that for personal reasons. I was responsible for a colleague's death—a *close* colleague. I came on holiday here partly purely as a holiday, and partly also as an obligement for old time's sake. I do not think they contacted you for sinister reasons. Simply that my friend in London, for whom I have a great affection, was hoping that the occurrence would not run me into trouble that I had not, as it were, contracted for.'

'*Volenti non fit iniuria?*' asked Mason.

'*Non volenti—fit iniuria,*' replied Jarvis, after a pause to work it out. 'I was—I am still—a watcher. That was all and is all. I took on no other risks.'

'Watching who?'

'That, I am not at liberty to disclose. But perhaps you have a private number just in case something interesting which I could pass on emerges in any conversation or discussion I might have. I dare say there will be some discussion. After all, it has all been very unexpected.'

'You are sure it was unexpected?'

'As sure as I can be.'

'How sure is that?'

'As sure as I can be.'

Mason gave him a number.

'If I find that there has been some criminal activity here by your friends,' he said, 'you can tell them from me that I will hound them to hell and past it. We don't work like that in my understanding of the policing of this country.'

'My friends do not work like that,' said Jarvis.

'But do you know them all? Would you be able to speak for all?'

'No.'

Mason sighed. 'Well,' he said, 'let's just hope that we find some other explanation for what has gone on. I still have some illusions.'

'So have I,' Jarvis replied.

SEVEN: SUNDAY

1

During breakfast, which Jarvis shared with his three friends, Phillipson came into the room. He came across to their table.

'I think,' he said, speaking to Jarvis, 'that if I remember right, I offered you a lift in to church this morning. I'm afraid I will have to withdraw the offer. There has been too much going on, and I cannot afford the time.'

'Surely,' replied Jarvis. 'I quite understand. I was going to see you after breakfast to say that I would go in on my own. I thought you would be up to the eyes.'

Phillipson blew out his cheeks and fluttered his hands. 'It has been pretty grim, with various members of the Trust wanting to be kept up to date, and so on. Thanks for understanding.' He went out into the kitchen.

'Are you going to church?' asked Kate Greenway.

'Yes,' said Jarvis, wondering whether to extend an invitation, but Dunne jumped in.

'I cannot see anything in that myself. I can see the urge, given recent events. They bring unpleasant thoughts to mind, but I never was at a church which helped. Pious words, but no real help.'

'It works for me,' replied Jarvis. He looked at his watch. 'In fact, I had better get a move on. It seems the local minister has to do a service at another church as well, two services in one morning. So the one in the village is at half past ten. The next is at twelve-fifteen a couple of miles away.'

'That wouldn't take him long to travel,' said Dunne.

Jarvis laughed. 'Maybe he preaches long to fill the time. He left to collect his coat.

When he came downstairs to the vestibule he found Kate waiting for him, dressed for going out.

'Can I come with you?' she said.

As they went into the churchyard Kate shivered, and not from the cold, but she stopped, as Jarvis had done, at the black gravestone just round the corner of the path beside the church. It attracted attention. A fresh red rose was in the vase.

'So far from home,' she said. 'But someone cares.'

Jarvis nodded, re-reading the inscription. He felt a thought begin at the back of his head. It would not come forward.

It was a good service. The minister was mindful of what had happened within his parish, and it seemed his preaching programme had that morning taken him to 1 *Corinthians* 15, the 'Resurrection' chapter. Not only Jarvis felt himself searched, challenged, and then strengthened by what was said.

As they entered the church, which was fairly full by the time they had arrived, both Jarvis and Kate were conscious of a number of people looking at them. Jarvis was not sure whether this was the usual curiosity of a congregation regarding strangers, or whether speculation was running that they had come 'from where it had happened'. At the end, however, when they rose to go, there was no awkwardness. The minister had in prayer spoken of 'those amongst us who had gone through trying experiences in recent days', and clearly the congregation had made the connection. At any rate, Kate was approached by a matronly woman, while her large, red-faced husband welcomed Jarvis to the church.

'We really ought to say hello to the minister,' said Jarvis at length, realizing how time was passing, and he took Kate by the elbow.

As they moved up the aisle, however, Kate stopped short.

Jarvis gave her elbow a nudge, but she demurred, and Jarvis followed her eyes. A man, head bent, was in the back pew. It was Dunne.

He seemed to feel their gaze, looked up and got up. His face was solemn as he waited for them to reach him.

'I went for a walk, and then felt I had to come,' he said. 'So I walked in. I'm glad I did.'

At the door Kate and Dunne shook the minister by the hand and went on. Jarvis chatted to him for a minute or so, thanking him for the service and what they had got out of it. The minister spoke briefly about the tragedies, saying that you never knew what a week might bring, and that, yes, he had recognized Jarvis from Tuesday evening. He was pleased they had been helped. Then Jarvis joined the others who were waiting for him. Kate was looking again at the black gravestone.

The rubicund gentleman and his wife came past.

'Interesting, that one,' he called. 'She worked up at the house. Where you are staying?'

Jarvis's thought stirred again, this time not so far back in his head, but still unclear.

As the three got into the car, Jarvis apologized.

'I need to make a phone-call,' he said. 'It won't take long.'

Between the car and the phone his thought came clear.

The phone conversation did not take long. He was quickly put through to George Appleby, who had come in to take his call, and succinctly he reported the events of the day before.

'Now, George,' he said. 'I have three questions, and must at least have answers to the first and the last.'

Appleby answered the first, said that he was not at liberty to answer the second and that in any event it was no longer a matter of any importance. As to the third, he promised a swift answer.

'I'll tell you what I think,' said Jarvis. 'You could phone me through to Ebony House and simply say "yes" or "no". But I know what I think, though I don't like it.'

'Go ahead,' said Appleby.

Jarvis outlined the thought which had come to him.

'I'll phone when I can,' said Appleby. 'Should I inform anyone else?'

'Not immediately,' said Jarvis. 'But if there is need to—and you would recognize that need—Superintendent Mason is your man. He looks like Satan, but smiles like an angel.'

'I thought Satan himself was good at that,' said Appleby, and put the phone down.

EIGHT: MONDAY

1

Monday was to be their last day. On the Sunday afternoon Superintendent Mason had indicated that everyone who was left at Ebony House was free to go. Some left immediately, but for various reasons others decided to wait until the Monday.

That morning, Dunne, Greenway and Mather decided they would wait till after lunch when the roads might be quieter, and elected to pass the time by going into Birley to seek out Jarvis's bookshop.

'After all,' said Mather with a laugh, 'it just might be that the place has not been pillaged. There are books more valuable than musty old law tomes.'

They invited Jarvis to go in with them, but he demurred. He had arranged a fishing lesson with Phillipson.

'I promised myself that I would conquer this business of the fly this holiday,' he said with a grin. 'So I'm going to give it another try. Besides, I want there to be something to look for next year in that shop.'

So it was agreed, and the three set off in Dunne's large, and somewhat decrepit, car.

They fished Ranald's Pool. Things went technically well, although nothing was biting. Jarvis found that he was beginning to master the technique of drifting the fly on the wind, and allowing it to settle in the right place for the current to bring it down to where the fish might be lurking. Phillipson was pleased with his progress.

After an hour or so they paused, sitting on adjacent boulders. Phillipson took out his fly case, and sat rearranging the delicate contents, and clipping off one or two spoiled flashes.

It was peaceful and pleasant. Jarvis decided to float another fly.

'Why did you do it?' he said, in Polish.

There was no reply. Jarvis turned slightly, not to look at Phillipson, but so that he was conscious of him in his peripheral vision. Phillipson was staring at him.

Jarvis repeated the question, this time turning to look directly at Phillipson. The man's knuckles were white, gripping the fly-case. Then he dropped a hand to the gaff which lay beside him on the grass, but did not pick it up. He brought his hand back, and cradled the case between them, tension running out of him.

Phillipson spoke; in English, but in answer to the question.

'It was opportunity.' Then, after a pause: 'Which I regret.'

'I was the agent of justice,' he went on. His hands now opened and spread. The case fell to the grass. His eyes were pleading. He stood up. So did Jarvis.

'Tell me,' said Jarvis. 'It will do you good.'

Phillipson almost smiled his crooked smile at that. 'Confession is good for the soul, you mean.'

'Something like that.'

'What do you want to know?'

'Why? How did you find out about Benedict?'

'His number. What do you know?'

'Maria Antonovitch, widow of Philip Antonovitch,' said Jarvis.

'Yes,' said Phillipson. 'I understand. It was an impulse to honour my father when I wanted to join the Navy. Philip's son. Was that the clue?'

'One of them.'

Phillipson looked closely at him, and then relaxed. 'One of them,' he said. 'One of them. And I thought I might get away with it.' He shook his head. 'What were the others?' he asked.

'A hunch, the content of some of that bible-study and your reaction to it, and a few questions on the phone. Tell me about it.'

Phillipson flexed his fingers several times, then spoke in a low voice.

'It was four years ago, when he first came here. My mother acted as maid. I do not think anyone suspected that we were related. She recognized him. She told me later that she had recognized him immediately, but that she said nothing till she was sure. That was the second evening, when she served his table. Close up, hearing him speak, was proof.

'I was at the table too. Myself, Professor Milton and some guest speaker they had invited.

'My mother was serving at the time. It was the potatoes, I remember. I was sitting opposite Benedict, and she was putting the potato dish on the table. She let it fall. There was quite a fuss, and in the confusion I saw she had gone white. She shook her head at me, I remember, and I said something about her rheumatic hands finding hot dishes a problem.' Tears welled up in his eyes. 'Later that night she told me.'

'Told you what?'

'He had been a trusty, a guard at Majdanek. He had, stories said, joined the Nazis, but was barred from Army service. I don't know whether that was policy, as he was a Pole, or whether it was his club foot. But he was a brute. They called him Caligula in the camp.'

'That was one of his nicknames here too,' said Jarvis quietly.

'And he had a stick. He used to hit anyone within range. You saw him with the plants beside the path?'

Jarvis nodded.

There was a tense silence. At length Jarvis sighed. 'You should have contacted Special Branch, or the Foreign or Home Offices, or even your MP.'

'If I had denounced him, what good would it have done? Would he have been sent back to Germany or Poland? Would there have been another of those drawn-out trials, and some nominal sentence? I had no real proof now. My mother is dead.'

Jarvis thought it out. If Benedict had been denounced, would there have been enough proof?

'What did you find out over there?' he asked, jerking a thumb roughly eastwards.

'On my fishing trips?'

'I don't think they do much fly-fishing in the lower Carpathians.'

'Enough,' said Phillipson.

'Then why not report it? Why kill?'

'Opportunity. Conviction. I was the hand of God.'

Jarvis waited and Phillipson resumed.

'It was that number he showed you that night. You remember he took off his jacket?'

'I remember.'

'Do you think that that tattoo made it easier for him to get over here?'

'It's a possibility.'

'That number, that passport, that stamp of approval . . .' He stopped, looked away, and then looked back. He took a step closer and looked deep into Jarvis's eyes.

'It was my mother's number,' he said.

The two men stood for long minutes together, then Phillipson asked a question.

'Why are you here? And so knowledgeable?'

Jarvis did not reply. Phillipson continued. 'You are still on the books. I wondered about you.'

'Me?'

'I was asked some time ago to let someone know if certain persons were coming to stay. Benedict was one. And, shortly after I did, you booked in.'

'You read much into coincidence.'

'You follow my reasoning too well,' said Phillipson. 'Deny it.'

There was a brief silence.

'That means, I suppose,' said Phillipson, 'that there is no escape.'

Jarvis was silent. Then he spoke. 'There is a belief in certain quarters that Professor Benedict was involved in recruiting, talent-spotting, watching for those who might be sympathetic and aiming at a career within the Civil Service. I find it incredible, having met the man. But steps were taken a year or so ago to deal with that situation, as could be seen from certain transfers within certain ministries. None involved had done anything, so far as we know, but it was felt proper that these steps should be taken. Where the transferees protested certain checks were made and in certain instances proposed transfers did not ocur.'

'But you,' said Phillipson. 'You were made an academic to track him?'

'No,' said Jarvis shortly. 'I am an academic by choice.' He sighed. 'You are right, of course,' he added. 'I was in the business, but something I was involved in went horribly wrong, and I retired.'

'But you never go on the inactive list,' said Phillipson.

'When someone heard that I was moving in the same circles, it was suggested to me that I should keep an eye on Benedict, just in case something useful turned up.'

'Ah.' Phillipson seemed to relax.

'Scores of able students passed through his hands, and it made some sort of sense. And he made regular visits back east, despite his professed distaste for it—the memories it held.'

'But was he not checked by your people? That would have done the job.'

'He was checked, but the records of the camp he claimed to have been in were missing.

'Yes,' said Phillipson. 'That is what I found too. The

Jewish Agency could not help either. It was all a blank.'

'Who was he?' Jarvis asked.

'His name was Czerny,' said Phillipson in a dreamy voice.
'At least, that is what my mother said, and it is the name he
responded to when I challenged him. I don't know where
he came from, but he claimed to come from a small village
which was erased in the fighting on the Eastern Front. There
was no one to disprove what he said, though there were
some rumours. But they were ashamed of them. It took a
lot of drinks before they would let slip anything about him.'

'Czerny,' said Jarvis. 'I'll have that checked.'

'No point,' said Phillipson. 'I checked with the Jewish
Agency, and they have no record of such. It seems he was
lucky. No one alive remembered him, or knew his name or
something.'

'Except your mother.'

'And me.' Phillipson sat down on the boulder and buried
his face in his hands a moment. Then looked up. 'It was
that number that did it,' he said. 'In my mind I can
understand. It was camouflage. I can see him, terrified . . .
the world collapsing around him . . . the tattoo the token
for freedom. But that came later.

'I knew that every morning he went a walk up the river.
When I found him, he was on that outcrop above the Pot.
I called him "Czerny". He turned. Fear was in his face.
Then he saw that it was me, and he turned back. "Beautiful
morning," he said, in that arrogant voice of his. He was
tapping his walking stick against his leg. And I thought of
that man, who had been a guard, guarding my mother, and
who had taken her number for his safety . . . accidentally,
no doubt—I realize that now. But then, it was simply he
. . . and my mother. The gaff was in my hand.' He dropped
his hands and stood erect. 'I buried it away up in a peat
bog up there,' he said, pointing to the hills above the
valley.

'In Mary's Mire?'

'Yes.'

'So you went looking for Benedict that morning with your gaff in your hand.'

'Yes. It seemed to me that if I found him, it was guidance that I was to be the Avenger of Blood.'

'Vengeance is mine, says the Lord.'

'I know that now,' said Phillipson softly. 'I wish I had not . . .'

'What about Huntley?'

'I do not know anything about that. That is why it was such a shock. I believe that Mason thinks he was killed by the other one . . .'

'Earlston.'

'Earlston, who then committed suicide.'

'Perhaps.'

Phillipson sighed, and began to pack up his gear. Jarvis did so as well.

Together they climbed the fishers' path to the upper path, coming out beside the seat from which Jarvis had watched Benedict those seven days before. At the top Phillipson dropped his rod, gaff and bag.

'Give me a few minutes,' he said.

Jarvis settled himself on the seat. He watched the breeze play with the birches on the opposite slope. A water wagtail bobbed its way up the boulders towards the linn, up past where Huntley had lain.

He mused in the warming sunshine. Deeply he regretted the week. Benedict's death. Now he would never give him that Lewis citation, or be able to penetrate behind that crusty exterior. But what sort of a man had be been? Were the suspicions justified? Had he been a guard, as Phillipson had said? Did London know anything of that?

Slowly he reviewed that last night's conversation about the Pool of Time—whatever happened he would always call it that. What had Benedict told him to read? *Into*

That Darkness by . . . was it Sereny? That was right. Gitta
Sereny.

His mind wound down, and he gave himself to the sun
and the breeze.

After a time he heard footsteps. Phillipson was coming
back. He stood to wait for him.

Phillipson smiled as he came up. 'I'll go and see Mason
this afternoon,' he said.

2

Early that afternoon Jarvis found Dunne and Kate Greenway loading cases into Dunne's car.

'Oh,' said the girl. 'I am glad. I was just up to your room
looking for you. I wanted to thank you.'

'For what?' asked Jarvis.

'For . . . for . . . You've been a great help to us,' she
replied. She went slightly red. 'It's not official yet,' she went
on. 'But Jim and I are getting married.'

'Congratulations, or felicitations—whichever it should
be. I haven't known either of you very long, but that looks
like a good idea to me,' said Jarvis. To his great surprise,
and not a little confusion, she reached up and kissed him.

'Steady,' said Dunne. 'I might change my mind.'

'No, you won't,' said Jarvis. 'Not if you have any sense.'

Mather came out, carrying his case.

'You've heard,' he said with a grin, looking from Dunne
to Jarvis, to Greenway and then back to Jarvis.

'Yes,' said Jarvis. 'And I approve.'

'So do I,' said Mather.

'We had better get going,' said Dunne. 'See you at that
eatery—what is it?—sixty miles down the road?'

The two got into Dunne's car, and drove off. Jarvis waved
them out of sight.

'They'll do,' said Mather quietly, as they vanished into
the beech tunnel. 'What are you going to do?' he asked.

'I've got another day,' said Jarvis.

'Lucky you,' said Mather, looking round. 'In other circumstances, this is a great place.'

'Yes.'

'I was looking for the Commander just now to say so, and to thank him,' said Mather, opening the boot of his car and putting the case into it.

'I think he has gone in to Birley on business.'

'Oh. Pity. Perhaps you will pass on my thanks, personal and corporate.'

'I'll do that when I see him.'

'I'm likely to be organizing our bash here next year,' said Mather. 'Milton has indicated that he wants shot of that duty, especially given what has happened this time. If I let you know, might you think of coming?'

'I'm not eligible.'

'If I am running it, and I say you are, you are,' replied Mather. 'And Milton will agree. You two got on well. Besides, remember what we were saying that night about too many people sheltering behind the walls of their disciplines? It's very true. I would like you to come and do a paper for us. A draught of cold legal air might do us good. And I'm not sure whether I mean "draught"—measure, or "draught"—gale.'

'That might be interesting,' said Jarvis. 'I'm all in favour of cross-fertilization. But will you come back here?'

'Yes,' said Mather stoutly. 'I like it here.' He swept an arm round—so like Benedict, Jarvis thought—indicating the whole, the pastureland in front, the cawing rooks, the greens, the blues in the sky, the breathy cows, the House itself.

'Can I drop you a note in a week or so?'

'Fine,' said Jarvis.

Mather got into his car, gave a wave, and then he too was gone down that leafy tunnel.

Jarvis looked at his watch. It was half past two. He

straightened himself deliberately from a slouch, and looked round taking in all the scenery, storing it away in that section of his mind where he held loved vistas. He sighed briefly, and went into Ebony House.

In the vestibule he met Anderson, who offered to take him down to the river and sort out once and for all what was wrong with his technique with the fly.

'Thanks,' said Jarvis. 'But I think the river has too many memories for me just now. I'll go a walk up the top of the valley instead, if you don't mind.'

'Funny bloke,' Anderson said shortly afterwards to the cook. 'He was out this morning with the Commander on the river. What about his memories then, eh?'